Boing. He thought it made a rather interesting sound as he dropped to the kitchen floor.

"Oh, my God, *Simon*!" The frying pan clattered onto the table as Frankie knelt on the floor next to him. "Si, are you all right?"

She leaned close to run her fingers lightly across his head, searching for the spot where she'd hit him.

Despite the bump on his head, it felt sinfully good. It was entirely possible that he'd died and gone to heaven.

"I better get you some ice," Frankie said.

He didn't need any ice. Not for his head anyway. It was other parts of his anatomy that could use cooling down. Her hand gently stroked the side of his face, and his cheek pressed against the softness of her belly. . . . Oh, this was too good an opportunity to pass up.

Simon let his eyelids flutter shut.

"Oh, no." Frankie said, worry in her voice. "You're not supposed to go to sleep with a head injury. Come on, you better sit up."

Simon let her pull him up, but then wobbled slightly so that she'd have to hold him tightly. She did, her breasts pressed against his chest, her arms around his back, her thighs gripping his hips. It felt too good. He couldn't keep a strangled sound of pleasure from escaping.

"Does it hurt that bad?"

Hurt? Not exactly . . .

WHAT ARE *LOVESWEPT* ROMANCES?

They are stories of true romance and touching emotion. We believe those two very important ingredients are constants in our highly sensual and very believable stories in the LOVE-SWEPT line. Our goal is to give you, the reader, stories of consistently high quality that may sometimes make you laugh, sometimes make you cry, but are always fresh and creative and contain many delightful surprises within their pages.

Most romance fans read an enormous number of books. Those they truly love, they keep. Others may be traded with friends and soon forgotten. We hope that each LOVESWEPT romance will be a treasure—a "keeper." We will always try to publish

LOVE STORIES YOU'LL NEVER FORGET
BY AUTHORS YOU'LL ALWAYS REMEMBER

The Editors

Loveswept ® 817

THE KISSING GAME

SUZANNE
BROCKMANN

BANTAM BOOKS
NEW YORK · TORONTO · LONDON · SYDNEY · AUCKLAND

THE KISSING GAME

A Bantam Book / December 1996

ISBN 0-553-44546-4

Published simultaneously in the United States and Canada

Bantam Books are published by Bantam Books, a division of Bantam Dou-
bleday Dell Publishing Group, Inc. Its trademark, consisting of the words
"Bantam Books" and the portrayal of a rooster, is Registered in U.S. Patent
and Trademark Office and in other countries. Marca Registrada. Bantam
Books, 1540 Broadway, New York, New York 10036.

PRINTED IN THE UNITED STATES OF AMERICA

OPM   0 9 8 7 6 5 4 3 2 1

For Carolee

ONE

"Hello?"

"Simon? Please tell me that Leila's there!"

After a brief silence, Simon Hunt's familiar voice said, "I could tell you that, Francine, but I'd be lying. My sister's not home right now. She and her future husband went to their third meeting with the caterers. If you ask me, this wedding thing is getting way out of hand."

Frankie Paresky closed her eyes and swore silently. "Simon, look, I need your help." She spoke quickly, not allowing her best friend's older brother time to speak, let alone a chance to refuse her. "I'm over at the airport. A charter flight just came in and I picked up the fare—only to find out that this man has come to Sunrise Key to see *me*. I asked him where he was headed, and he gave me *my* address. I need you to do me a humongous favor—I need you to go over to my office and unlock the door. When I drop this guy off, let him into the waiting room and stall him until I can come in the back and change my clothes."

Simon was laughing at her, damn him. "You mean you don't want a client to know that you moonlight as one of this island's most illustrious cabdrivers?"

"There's nothing wrong with my earning a few extra bucks driving a cab," Frankie said, "but . . . I really want this guy to take me seriously."

"And you think he's going to take you seriously if you quickly change into your trench coat and fedora and pretend he doesn't know you're the same person who drove him from the airport?"

"Will you please stop with the trench-coat jokes for once?" Frankie demanded. "I don't even own a trench coat, and you know it."

"I thought you were issued one when you graduated from private eye school."

"Thanks a million, Hunt. Lord, why did I even bother—"

"Relax, Francine. I'm going to help you. But are you sure you shouldn't just be honest with this man? Tell him who you really are?"

Over the crystal-clear telephone wires, Simon's voice sounded warm and rich and smooth, as if he were standing right behind her, his breath warm on the back of her neck. If Frankie turned around, she'd see him, his brilliant blue eyes gleaming with amusement, his elegant lips curving into a smile, his blond hair tousled by the soft ocean breeze. Frankie closed her eyes briefly, trying to rid her mind of that distracting image.

"He hasn't actually looked at me," she said. "He's tired, and I think the charter hop from the mainland made him airsick. Besides, I spent the morning at the beach and I'm wearing a baseball cap and sunglasses. I'm not even sure he realizes I'm a woman."

"Getting airsick doesn't make you blind," Simon pointed out. "You're hardly five feet tall, Paresky. I'd bet last month's profits that he knows you're a woman."

"I could be a sixteen-year-old boy—"

"No," Simon said decisively, "you could not."

Across the metal Quonset hut that served as the airport's shelter, the door to the men's room swung open and the man from the charter flight came out.

"I've got to go," Frankie said quickly. "Are you really going to help me?"

"You want me to unlock the door and stall, right? I'll go right over."

"Please don't blow this for me."

"I would have thought 'thank you' was the correct response."

"Thank you."

"You're going to owe me, Francine."

Frankie hung up the phone and hustled outside. She was sitting in the driver's seat of the cab before the man—her first off-island client—came out of the Quonset hut. She watched in the rearview mirror as he squinted and staggered slightly in the bright Florida sunshine. He used a folded white handkerchief to wipe sweat from his forehead as he carefully squeezed his big frame into the taxi's backseat.

He wasn't dressed for Sunrise Key's muggy tropical heat. Frankie guessed he was from Chicago, or some other midwestern city. Cleveland, perhaps. She'd seen on the TV news that the unseasonably hot April weather that was warming most of the East Coast and turning Florida into a steam bath hadn't moved as far west as Ohio. She'd put a heavy, lined raincoat into the backseat of the cab along with his luggage—he wouldn't have brought the raincoat if it hadn't been cold and wet where he'd come from.

Whoever he was, his initials were C.A.Q., and his luggage was leather and very, very expensive. Everything about this man, from his well-tailored wool business suit to his manicured fingernails, screamed money.

As Frankie pulled the cab out onto Airport Road, she felt a surge of anticipation. Frankie Paresky, Private Investigations, Inc., could certainly use an off-island client who had money.

She glanced at him in the mirror again as he leaned his head back against the seat and closed his eyes. He was a tall man, several inches over six feet, with the big, bearlike build of a former high school or college football player. It had been some years since he'd last played though—he was probably close to forty years old—and his once-muscular physique had softened quite a bit. His hair was brown and thinning slightly on top. His face was still handsome, with deep laugh lines around his eyes and mouth.

Why did this man need the services of a private investigator? And why was he in such a hurry that he couldn't take the time to stop at the hotel and recover from his obviously unpleasant flight before he got down to business?

Frankie was dying to ask him some questions—any questions that might give her a clue as to his purpose for being on the island, but she was afraid to speak and draw attention to herself. The answers to her questions were going to have to wait.

As she took the left turn onto Ocean Avenue, heading toward the cluster of shops and offices that made up the downtown area of Sunrise Key, Frankie tried to remember which clean clothes were hanging in her closet. Usually when she was working a case she wore jeans shorts and a T-shirt. But she had a feeling that such casual attire would not impress this man, who wore a designer necktie, gold cuff links, and Italian shoes. On the other hand, if she changed into one of her two dresses—which she knew were clean because she rarely wore them—she might come across as being too feminine. As loath as she was to put on long pants in this ninety-five-degree weather, she was going to have to go with her khakis and a white button-down shirt.

Frankie hoped Simon had the good sense to turn the air conditioner to its coldest setting.

She turned onto Harcourt Street and pulled the cab into the drive of the beach house that served as both her home and her office. Her potential client opened his eyes and dug into his jacket pocket for his wallet.

"How much do I owe you?" he asked.

"There's a five-dollar minimum per trip." Frankie pulled her baseball cap down over her eyes and made her voice lower, scratchier. Simon's Jeep was parked across the street, bless him. He'd come through for her.

You're going to owe me, Francine. Simon's bedroom-soft voice echoed in her mind, leaving her to speculate on the limitless possibilities for payback. A vision of Simon Hunt, all lean, tan muscles, golden-blond hair, and gleaming white smile, sprawled across her queen-sized bed made Frankie roll her eyes in self-disgust. As if she'd ever get involved with the man who was Sunrise Key's answer to Don Juan. Simon dated the women who came to the island on vacation. They stayed for a week, and then they bid him a teary farewell. Occasionally one of them would stay longer—much to Simon's dismay. After two weeks he'd get that haunted look in his eyes, and after three weeks, tops, the woman would leave the island, usually brokenhearted.

No, Frankie was much too smart to add herself to Simon's list of conquests. Sure, he was one of the most attractive men she'd ever met, but she'd successfully buried that attraction for years. And years and years and years. She'd known him for close to forever. She was best friends with his sister. She'd practically grown up in his house. His mom and dad were the closest thing to parents she'd ever had. No, indeed. Simon was—and would remain—her friend and only her friend.

The man in the backseat handed her a ten-dollar bill. "Keep the change," he told her.

As soon as he had closed the door behind him, Frankie backed out of the driveway and took off down the street. She made a quick left onto Ocean Avenue, then another left on the side street that ran parallel to Harcourt. She parked the cab in front of the house whose backyard connected to hers and jumped out. A dog barked, startling her as she ran alongside the cottage. She put on a burst of speed.

The thick bushes that separated the two backyards were more difficult to get through than Frankie had anticipated. She pushed and wriggled her way into her own yard, crawling on her belly in the soft dirt. And then she was up and running again. It took but a second to cross her small yard and clamber up the back deck, onto the rail, and up onto the roof above the kitchen.

The only way into her upstairs apartment was through her downstairs office—or through the second floor windows.

But she'd forgotten to ask Simon to make sure she left the window in her bedroom unlocked. Please, she prayed silently, please be open.

Locked. It was locked. Damn!

But then the curtain moved, and Simon was there, unlocking the window. He opened both the glass and the screen and reached out, giving Frankie a hand, pulling her inside.

She stumbled, and he caught her easily, his arms solid around her.

"Whoa," Simon murmured, his mouth mere inches from her ear. "Slow down, Francine. You're going a mile a minute."

She was. Her heart was pounding, and she couldn't seem to catch her breath. The fact that she was pressed full against Simon's hard, lean body was making matters worse. Lord, save her from herself.

Simon didn't realize that he had the ability to make Frankie's pulse race, and she was damned if she was going to let him find out. She pulled free from his embrace. "You're supposed to be downstairs, distracting the client."

"I left him in the outer office, sipping iced tea. You're supposedly on the phone long distance with another client, so you've got a few minutes at least. Oh, yeah, and he gave me this." Simon held out a tastefully lettered business card.

Frankie took it from him. Clayton Alan Quinn, she read, Attorney at Law, from the firm of Quinn, Conners, Alberts & Maine, in Grosse Pointe, Michigan. The jeans shorts and a T-shirt would definitely remain in the dresser drawer.

She pulled off her soil-streaked T-shirt. The blue-and-white tank bathing suit she was wearing underneath was dry. It was scratchy from salt and sand, but she could live with that. "Get my khakis and a white shirt from the closet, will you, Si?"

She crossed to the tiny adjacent bathroom and began washing the dirt from the garden off her hands and elbows. She glanced into the mirror as Simon opened her closet door. Instead of finding her slacks and shirt, he pulled out the dress with the tiny blue-flowered print.

"Francine." He held it up so that she could see it in the bathroom mirror. "Aliens have invaded your home, leaving behind strange garments—the likes of which your closet has never before seen."

"It's a dress, Simon."

"I *know* what it is. But barring Halloween, I don't think I've ever, in my entire life, seen you in a dress." He reached back into the closet and took out her green dress. "Yo, and what's this? Another dress? Now I'm really confused. Paresky, have you been wearing women's clothing on the sly?"

Toothbrush in her mouth, Frankie stuck her head out of the bathroom, trying her best to wither Simon with a single look. But he was at his most obnoxiously wither-proof, so she took the toothbrush from her mouth and explained. "I got the green dress three years ago for Evan Water's funeral. The blue was for Kim and Noah Kavanaugh's wedding—"

"Oh, man, what's *this*?" Simon lifted the protective plastic covering of the most decadent item in Frankie's closet—a dress that her best friend, Simon's sister Leila, had ordered her from the Victoria's Secret catalogue. It was minuscule and black and Leila had bought it despite the fact that Frankie had sworn up and down and over and across that she would never, ever, *ever* wear it.

Frankie quickly rinsed her toothbrush and her mouth, then hurried across the room, snatching the dress from Simon. "That's Leila's idea of a little joke."

She hung it as far back in the closet as she could reach, then quickly began the search for her slacks and shirt.

"Frankie, you know how you've been wanting to go up to Sarasota, to the ballet?"

"No one will go with me." Frankie pulled her khaki slacks off their hanger and tossed them onto her bed. She glanced at Simon, who was leaning against the wall, watching her, arms and ankles crossed. "Except for Leila, and she's not going to have any free time until after the wedding."

"I'll take you to the ballet," Simon said, "provided you wear that black dress."

"No way!"

He was completely serious. "I'll even take you to dinner at Chez Jean-Paul. Five-star gourmet cuisine . . . ?"

"That's a lot of trouble and expense to go to for a cheap laugh."

"Who said anything about laughing?"

"Yeah, right." Frankie found the shirt she wanted and pulled it on right over her bathing suit. She wriggled out of her shorts and stepped into the slacks, buttoning the shirt and tucking the tails in. She slipped her feet back into her sandals as she fastened the waistband and straightened her collar. A quick brush through her short dark hair and . . .

"How do I look?"

Simon had an odd look on his face, and at her words he snapped to attention, then squinted slightly. "You need a belt."

"No, I don't."

"Yes, you do. For Clayton Alan Quinn from Grosse Pointe, Michigan, you definitely need to wear a belt."

"Then you better lend me yours, 'cause I don't have a prayer of finding mine in the next few minutes."

"It'll wrap twice around your waist," Simon protested.

Frankie held out her hand. "Give it."

Simon started to unfasten his brown leather belt. "If I lend you this belt, you have to promise to wear that black dress someday soon."

"How about you lend me your belt and I promise I don't kill you?"

"I like my deal better." Simon handed her the belt.

It didn't wrap quite twice around her, but even on the tightest setting it was loose. But it looked better than empty belt loops.

"Just out of curiosity, Francine," Simon said, moving to block her way out of the room. "What *would* it take to get you to wear that dress?"

Frankie looked up into Simon's eyes. "Maybe not what. Maybe *who*."

"Not me, huh?"

Frankie snorted and pushed past him. "Definitely not you."

TWO

"Mr. Quinn, I'm Frankie Paresky. Sorry to keep you waiting, sir."

Simon watched as the big man pushed himself to his feet to shake Frankie's hand across her desk.

"*You're* Frankie Paresky?" Clayton Quinn's mouth curved up into a smile.

"Is there a problem?" Frankie bristled slightly as they both sat down.

"I was expecting someone—"

"Taller?" Simon supplied, coming all the way into the room and sitting down in the chair next to Quinn.

"Older," Quinn admitted.

Frankie turned to Simon. It was amazing how quickly the warm dark brown of her eyes could turn to ice. Even her warm southern drawl seemed chilly. "Simon, I'm sure Mr. Quinn would appreciate having a little privacy for this meeting—"

"Actually, it's okay by me if your assistant stays."

Quinn shot a friendly smile in Simon's direction. Simon had liked the man immediately, from the moment he'd first opened Frankie's door to him. "In fact, I'm here because I'm trying to track someone down, and the more people who know that I'm looking for this man, the better my chances are of finding him."

Simon felt Frankie glance in his direction again, and he knew that she wanted him to leave. But now he was doubly curious. He wanted to know who Quinn was looking for, and he wanted to see Frankie Paresky, Private Eye, in action.

He had to admit that she looked good. If he had just walked into the room, he'd have no idea that she was wearing a Speedo bathing suit and probably a small truckload of beach sand underneath her neatly conservative clothing. She looked sun-kissed and gorgeous as usual—her cheeks and delicate, slightly upturned nose a bit more rosy than the rest of her heart-shaped face.

Her short dark hair was probably salty from her trip to the beach, but it looked as if she'd spent quite a bit of time in front of the bathroom mirror with gel and a hair dryer to achieve that windswept look.

She looked every inch the professional, down to the yellow legal pad she'd pulled out of her desk drawer.

"Before we get into the details of your case," she said, opening a file drawer in her desk and taking out what looked like a standard contract form, "I'd like you to understand what my rates are. Seventy-five dollars an hour, one hundred dollars for travel hours and time over twelve hours per day. Should you decide to sign a contract with me today, I'll require a thousand-dollar retainer. In return, I'll provide you with a full accounting of my time, efforts, and expenses, plus all information I uncover in the course of this investigation."

Clayton Alan Quinn took out his checkbook, not batting an eye. "I'll write the retainer for five thousand," he said, "because I suspect you'll need more than a few days to find the fellow I'm looking for. In fact, if you can manage to get the job done in one week's time, I'll give you a ten-thousand-dollar bonus on top of your fee."

Simon heard Frankie's voice shake only a tiny bit. In fact, Quinn probably didn't even notice. "And if I get the job done in less than a week?"

Quinn laughed. "We'll work something out."

Frankie nodded. "Who exactly are you looking for, Mr. Quinn?"

"Clay," Quinn corrected her with a smile as he tore the check from his leather checkbook and placed it on the desk in front of her. "Please, call me Clay. I'm looking for a man named John."

Frankie slipped the check into the top drawer of her desk, not even glancing in Simon's direction. He knew that ten thousand dollars was more than half of her last year's earnings. How had she sat there with a straight face discussing ten-thousand-dollar bonuses?

Yet Clay seemed to believe that she was worth it. The real test was to come—when she actually had to solve the case. In less than a week's time.

Simon watched as she made a note on her pad. John. She looked up at Clay Quinn, her bottomless dark eyes wide. "John . . . who?"

Clay chuckled ruefully. "That's the problem. I don't know the man's last name."

Frankie sat back in her chair. "Maybe you'd better explain."

"I'm the executor of my great-aunt's will. She owned a vacation home here on Sunrise Key."

Frankie shot Simon a quick look, and he knew what she was thinking. They both knew everyone who owned property on the tiny island, and all of the homeowners were alive and healthy. Except for one . . .

"Is your great-aunt Alice Winfield?" Frankie asked, sitting forward.

"Yes, that's right."

"But she died more than eight years ago. We'd assumed her property here on the key had simply changed hands—"

"Eight years ago she had a massive stroke," Clay told Frankie. "She never fully recovered, and last month she finally died."

"She was alive until last month?" Frankie stared at Clay Quinn as if he were evil incarnate instead of the man who'd just handed her a five-thousand-dollar retainer. "Why was no one on Sunrise Key notified? Alice Winfield had friends here, Mr. Quinn—friends who would have written to her at the very least!"

Clay held up his hands as if to ward off a potential physical attack. "I'm sorry. I didn't even know Great-

Aunt Alice had a house down here until after she was gone."

Frankie turned to Simon, and he saw that she actually had tears in her eyes. Man, she was an emotional fireball. She always had been. Quick to accuse, quick to throw down a challenge, quick to the defense, quick to attack. But also equally quick to forgive and forget.

Gazing into her emotion-moistened brown eyes, Simon found himself wondering not for the first time what Frankie would be like in bed. Not for the first time? Hell, not even for the first time today. What it would be like to make love to Francine Paresky was something that he'd wondered almost every single day for the past twelve years. And lately it seemed as if he were wondering it with more and more frequency. Like when she startled him by stripping down to her bathing suit right in front of him, the way she had upstairs not more than a few minutes earlier. Like when he saw her walking toward him on Ocean Avenue. Or when she smiled. When he heard the husky sound of her laughter or the velvet-soft rise and flow of her southern accent. When he woke up in the morning. When he fell asleep at night . . .

"You remember Alice Winfield, don't you, Si?" she asked.

He could picture her in that sexy-as-hell black dress, the soft fabric clinging to her lithe body—an incredible body she was careful always to keep hidden beneath baggy T-shirts, loose shorts, and utilitarian bathing suits. He could picture her without the dress—her mouth hungry, her fingers in his hair, her body eager beneath his. . . .

"Yeah." He cleared his throat and shifted slightly in his seat. "Alice Winfield. Of course I remember her." More precisely, he remembered that she owned that huge Victorian house on Pelican Street, the one he'd suspected was loaded with the kind of well-cared-for, impeccably made old furniture that was the staple of his diet as an antiques dealer. He'd been dying to get inside that house for years. He should be thinking about *that*, not focusing on insane sexual fantasies. "She used to be a schoolteacher, right?"

"I used to go over and help her weed her garden," Frankie said. "I took care of it for her in the summer, when she was up north. She was the sweetest, kindest lady. If I had known she was still alive, I would have kept in touch."

"I didn't know her that well myself," Clay Quinn admitted. "But her husband apparently left her quite a fortune when he died, and she invested it well. Her estate is substantial, and she's been quite generous in distributing it among her relatives. She had no children of her own, you know."

Frankie nodded, her full attention on Quinn.

Simon caught himself staring at her again. Man, what was wrong with him? Sure, she was extraordinarily pretty—despite the fact that she usually dressed like a longshoreman. But so what? Hundreds of pretty women were walking up and down Sunrise Key's crescent-shaped beach right that very moment. And maybe that was his problem. Maybe it had simply been too long since he'd wined and dined—and seduced—one of the lovely visitors to this island. Tonight he'd go to the restaurant up at the resort, find himself a dinner date, and he wouldn't give Francine Paresky another thought.

"Alice wrote in her will that the property here on Sunrise Key be given to a man named John," Quinn was saying, "who vacationed down here for two weeks each spring for a period of about seven years in the late 1970s, early 1980s. According to Alice, he rented one of the cottages near her house on Pelican Street. Apparently, while his wife spent time on the beach, he helped Alice with odd jobs and repairs. She wrote that he never took a dime for all the work he did for her, and that he used to drop by in the evenings and play gin rummy. Alice wasn't sure she ever even knew his last name. She thought his wife's name was something like Lynn or Lana, and he had a son with some kind of slangy nickname. Biff or Buzz or—"

"Jazz?" Frankie asked.

Simon had to laugh. Didn't it figure? Maybe the notion of Frankie Paresky being a private investigator wasn't such an absurd one. After all, she knew everyone on the island—and apparently everyone who had ever visited the island too.

"I knew a boy named Jazz who vacationed here every spring for a number of years," Frankie continued. "I think I first met him when I was, I don't know, maybe twelve. The last time I saw him was the year I turned eighteen. He was on spring break from college—Boston University, I think it was. His family always rented one of the houses on Pelican Street."

"I can't believe you can remember some kid who was here only two weeks out of the year," Simon said.

Frankie flashed him a look. "Jazz was . . . memorable. I don't recall his last name, but I'm sure I've got it written down somewhere."

Jazz. The name—and the expression on Frankie's face—suddenly brought forward memories of an uncommonly good-looking teenage boy with sun-streaked brown hair and the wiry physique of a marathon runner. In fact, Simon could picture Jazz running along the beach, hand in hand with Frankie, laughing and gasping and collapsing on the sand to kiss her—long, slow, deep kisses that were heart-stopping even to watch. And God knows Simon *had* watched. That was the summer Frankie had turned eighteen—the summer Simon had realized that his little sister's best friend had grown from a scruffy kid into a dazzlingly beautiful woman. He couldn't keep his eyes off Frankie—even when she was with Jazz.

Simon had actually asked Frankie out that summer, but she didn't seem to notice him. She was totally wrapped up in that bastard Jazz—despite the fact that the kid had been gone for nearly two months.

"Is that where you intend to start the search?" Quinn asked. "By tracking down the son?"

"I think we're going to have to," Frankie told him. "If I remember correctly, Jazz was living with his mother and his stepfather. Jazz and John—if Jazz's stepdad really is the man we're looking for—wouldn't have the same last name." She took a manila file folder out from a drawer and wrote "Quinn" on the tab. "I'll also check with a friend of mine who works at the real estate office. Ten or twelve years is a long time ago, but she just might have rental records that go back that far for the houses on Pelican Street. Maybe we can find John's last name that way."

Quinn nodded. "I'll be staying at the Seaholm Resort until my flight out tomorrow evening. Let me know if you find anything."

"You're leaving so soon?"

He smiled ruefully. "I could stand a good vacation, but unfortunately, I've got business back home that won't wait. I didn't even have time to call you before I left Michigan. I apologize for showing up unannounced."

Frankie put her notes into the file and closed it. "Not a problem."

Clay Quinn glanced at his Rolex watch. "Would you mind calling a cab for me?"

Frankie froze. "Umm."

Simon knew what she was thinking. She was thinking that the island's one cab was parked over on the next block. She was thinking that even if she ran upstairs and changed back into her T-shirt and shorts and baseball cap, there was no way that Quinn wasn't going to recognize her as the cabdriver this time.

Simon came to her rescue. "I've got my Jeep right outside. Why don't you let me give you a lift up to the resort?"

"Well, thank you, I'd appreciate that." Quinn stood up, gathering his luggage and overcoat. He turned back to Frankie. "I forgot to mention—I'm going over to the house on Pelican Street tomorrow morning, if you'd like to come along. I'm not sure if there'll be any clues inside, but who knows?"

"What time?" Frankie asked.

"Nine o'clock?"

"I'll meet you over there."

"I'll be there too," Simon said.

Frankie smiled sweetly at Simon. Much, much too sweetly. "May I see you in the back room, please?" She turned to Clay. "Will you excuse us for just a moment?"

"Of course."

Simon followed Frankie down the hall and into the kitchen, watching as she closed the swinging door behind them.

"I appreciate your giving Clay Quinn a ride to the resort," she said in a low voice, "and I'll love you forever for being here for me this afternoon, but you are *not* my assistant or my sidekick or my *any*thing. Unless, of course, you want to help with the less glamorous work—like digging through the real estate records . . . ?"

"Nine o'clock tomorrow morning, the doors to number six Pelican Street are going to be opened for the first time in years." Simon tried to keep his voice low too, but he couldn't keep his excitement hidden. "Think of the treasures that could be inside!"

"It could be nothing but junk, Si."

"It could be priceless. It could be exactly what one of my clients is looking for."

"And it all belongs to this mysterious John," Frankie pointed out.

"You find this man John," Simon said, "and I'll get him to sell me Alice Winfield's antique furniture."

Frankie was looking up at him, the expression in her eyes unreadable. What was she thinking? He had no trouble with other women. Other women he could read like a book. But Frankie . . . she was a mystery.

"Look." Simon hoped he didn't sound as desperate as he felt. "All I want is to get into that house and take a look around. Let me show up tomorrow morning, and we'll be even. Clean slate. Full payback."

She didn't say a word. She just looked at him.

"Okay," he said. "I'll also go over to the real estate office with you this afternoon, help you sort through rental records. Then we'll *really* be even." He paused. "Please?"

Frankie smiled. "I'm wondering, if I just keep standing here, not saying anything, will you eventually offer me the deed to your house."

"I don't think taking a look inside Alice Winfield's house is quite worth the deed to mine," Simon said. "But I'd appreciate it if you could give me a few minutes to think it over." He paused for one tenth of a second. "All right, I'll throw that in too."

Frankie laughed, shaking her head. "You're impossible to refuse."

"You were doing a damn good job of it a few minutes ago."

Frankie pushed open the kitchen door, gesturing for him to lead the way out. "I'll meet you at the real estate office in half an hour."

THREE

"The rental records weren't computerized until 1989," Maia Fox told Frankie, pulling down several file boxes and a great deal of dust from the real estate office's basement storage shelves. She carried one of the boxes to the large table set up under several rows of bright fluorescent lights. A copy machine stood ready and waiting nearby. "The previous owner recorded everything by hand, in record books. This box holds the books dated 1971 to 1975. I'm not sure how complete they are, or if they'll even have the information you're looking for. But if the house was rented through this office, there should be *some* record of a payment transaction in these books. Those from 1976 to '80 and '81 to '85 are over there."

"Thanks, Maia," Frankie told the sweet-faced real estate agent.

"Let me know if you need anything else," Maia said with a smile. Her smile faded as she looked at

Simon. Giving a little sniff, she went up the rickety basement stairs.

Frankie turned to Simon, one eyebrow raised.

Simon opened the file box and pulled out the first account book, pretending to be intrigued by its fake leather cover.

"Are you going to tell me what that was about?" Frankie asked. "Or am I going to have to guess?"

Simon knew enough not to play dumb. He smiled ruefully. "She hasn't forgiven me."

"Should I even bother to ask why?"

"We had something of a short-lived affair a few years ago."

"Oh, Simon, you didn't."

Simon actually had the good grace to look ashamed. "She came by with a casserole and some comfort after Dad's funeral. I wasn't thinking clearly—I passed on the casserole and took the comfort. I should have done it the other way around, because she was looking for something a little longer-term. I can plead not guilty by reason of temporary insanity due to grief, but it's true, I should have recognized that Maia was a mistake right from the start."

"Is there anyone in town that you *haven't* slept with?" Frankie asked. "No—forget it. I don't really want to know the answer to that question."

She sat down and began leafing through the second account book. The pages were organized by month. The rental properties were listed down the left-hand side. There were four on Pelican Street that were rented with any regularity. And—hip hooray!—the renters' names, addresses, and telephone numbers were listed in neat spidery handwriting in the right-hand column.

"Here's how we're going to do it," she said. "We'll make copies of the pages dated February through May that list any Pelican Street rentals. Highlight in yellow the Pelican Street lines on the photocopy and make sure the month and year of the rental are clear on the page. And if the renter is named John, mark it with red."

"You know, Francine, I haven't slept with everyone in town."

Frankie looked up. He was still standing there, holding the ledger book, his face serious as he watched her steadily. She stood up and crossed to the copy machine, lined up the page on the glass surface, closed the lid, and pushed the start button.

"It's really not my business if you have."

"I know it seems as if I use women—"

"Seems? Something tells me Maia would laugh if she heard you say that."

"I don't," Simon protested. "At least I don't mean to. I've never made a woman any promises—and I certainly never made any to Maia. For God's sake, it wasn't as if she didn't know me. Did she honestly think that one night with her was going to change my entire life?"

"Yeah," Frankie said wryly. "She probably did. And I hate to break it to you, but there's probably more than one woman out there who interpreted your actions as unspoken promises."

"*Unspoken* promises?" Simon let out his breath in a half-laugh of exasperation. "Well, that's their problem."

"It's your problem too." Frankie flipped through the account book and found May. "Maia thinks you're the kind of man who breaks his promises. I'm sure she's not alone in her thinking."

The copy machine whirred again.

Simon shook his head. "If I promised to be faithful, I would be. If I asked someone to marry me, I'd hold those vows sacred."

His blue eyes were lit with intensity, and Frankie found herself believing him. Of course she believed him. Simon would keep his promises. But the promise of a lasting relationship was one he'd never, ever make, not in a million years.

"I just haven't met a woman that I'd want to spend the rest of my life with," he continued. "I haven't been in a relationship that hasn't made me feel . . . hell, I don't know . . . trapped." He looked down at the book he was still holding in his hands and cleared his throat. Frankie found herself holding her breath, waiting to hear what he had to say. "Everyone thinks all I do is have fun, but you know what? I'm not having so much fun anymore. All of my friends are getting married and having babies, and I'm still dating their little sisters. At the rate I'm going, sometimes I feel as if it's just a matter of time before I start dating their daughters. I'm tired of it, Frankie. But every time I'm with a woman and I ask myself if maybe she could be the one,

I come up with a four-foot-long list of reasons why I should turn and run. So I run."

Simon looked up at her, waiting for some kind of response, wanting to hear her opinion and advice. It was odd—Frankie had known Simon since his family had moved onto the key when he was a teenager. Through the years, despite the fact that she was his sister Leila's friend, they'd had quite a number of these soul-baring heart-to-hearts, and Frankie had never failed to be surprised by the faith and trust Simon put in her friendship.

She knew for certain that his conversations with whoever his current lady-love was never went this deep. Still, there were times—like when Frankie watched him across a crowded restaurant as he flirted with a dinner date, drawing the palm of his lover's hand to his lips, or when he slow-danced with some lovely young thing at the Rustler's Hideout—that she would have traded the heart-to-hearts for a bit more body contact.

But not anymore, Frankie reminded herself. She had been hired to find Jazz. How about *that* for destiny? She was going to be paid—and paid well—to find the one boy she'd never managed to forget.

But if Jazz was so unforgettable, why was she so damned distracted by Simon's picture-perfect looks, by his elegant cheekbones and perfectly shaped nose, by his neon-blue eyes and his graceful lips, by his thick blond hair and to-die-for body . . . ?

"Maybe you have to stop thinking of yourself as being trapped," she told him, pulling her gaze away from his. "*Secure* is a much nicer word for a permanent relationship. And maybe if you focus on what you've got rather than what you can't have . . ."

"Easier said than done."

"You know, I predict you're going to meet a woman you simply cannot live without," Frankie said. "You're going to take one look at her, realize that she's your soul mate, and you're going to promise her the sun and the moon."

"Soul mate, huh? You're a hopeless romantic, Paresky. Man, who would've thought?"

Frankie turned back to the copy machine, opening the lid and turning the ledger's page. She pressed the start button and the machine hummed. "So what if I am?"

Simon pushed himself up so he was sitting on the table. Frankie had her back to him as she diligently made copy after copy from the record book. "Tell me about this Jazz guy that you're looking for. I didn't really know him, but I remember that you and he were hot and heavy for a while."

Frankie turned to look at him, and as usual, her eyes were unreadable. "I never went out with the kids who came down here for vacation," she said. "Except for Jazz. He was different. He was the kind of boy who read classic literature and watched movies with subtitles. He could recite poetry and play the piano, and he picked me a bouquet of wildflowers every time we were together. I never knew anyone like him before." She smiled. "He was my first."

"First lover?"

Her smile turned to a disbelieving frown. "Lord, no. I was only eighteen. I wasn't ready for *that*. *He* was, but I wasn't. No, I meant he was my first kiss."

"At eighteen? Man, you *were* innocent."

She smiled again. "Yeah, I guess I was."

"So is he your 'soul mate'?"

Frankie leaned back against the copy machine, a flash of emotion in her eyes. "I don't know. Maybe. I mean, doesn't it seem odd that after all this time I should be hired to find him?"

"As if it's fate?"

"Exactly." She brought the copies to the table and took another ledger book. "Come on, don't just sit there. Highlight these."

"He's probably married." Simon slid off the table and down into a chair as he uncapped the yellow highlighting pen.

"Maybe he's not."

"Maybe it's just a coincidence that you're looking for him. Just because you bump into the guy again doesn't make him your soul mate. Look at you and me—we're together all the time. That doesn't make *us* soul mates."

Frankie snorted. "I should say not. Especially since I'm clearly last on your list of the women in town you'd like to seduce."

"What?"

She carried another stack of copies to the table. "Nothing. Never mind."

Simon caught her arm, tipping his chair back to gaze up at her. "Says who?" She wriggled to get free, but he wouldn't release her. "Where on earth did you ever get that idea?" he asked.

Frankie sighed, embarrassment tingeing her face. Up close like this, her skin was remarkably smooth and the faint pink of her blush made her look charmingly, delightfully sweet. Her eyes were lowered and her lashes looked as if they were a quarter of a mile long, thick and dark against her cheeks. She smelled good too. She'd showered while he was driving Clay Quinn up to the resort. Her hair was still slightly damp around the edges, and the sweet scent of her shampoo lingered. She'd changed back into her default uniform—baggy shorts and an old T-shirt—but Simon was well aware of the trim, compact, and totally feminine body she was hiding under her androgynous clothes.

She lifted her gaze, looking directly into his eyes, and Simon nearly fell over backward in his chair. It was as if she had touched him and the warmth of that touch had traveled down beneath his skin, tunneling throughout his entire body, causing every cell to tingle.

But she didn't seem to notice. She tugged again, trying to get her wrist free from his grasp. "I don't know why I said that," she admitted. "I mean, I'm *glad* that you think of me as a friend, not a . . . I mean, I'm not your type, so of course you wouldn't . . ."

"You think *I* think you're not my type?"

"Well, yeah." Frankie finally pulled away from him.

"What if I told you you were wrong, and that I

think an average of seven lustful thoughts about you every day?"

Frankie laughed, rubbing her wrist. "I'd laugh in your face and call you a liar."

"It's true."

Her dark eyes flashed. "Give me a break, Simon."

"Have I ever lied to you?"

She smiled slightly. "Probably."

Man, he was actually sitting there, flirting with Francine Paresky. He smiled back at her, silently challenging her not to be the first to look away. "Right now, for instance, I'm having seven lustful thoughts simultaneously."

She glanced away, but only for a second. "Only seven?" she said, lifting one eyebrow a bit.

Man, she was actually flirting back. Simon had always thought that she thought he wasn't *her* type. Except for that one time, nearly a dozen years ago, he'd never even dared to ask Frankie out. Oh, he pretended to ask her out, like when he found that incredible black dress in her closet. But neither of them ever took that seriously. Maybe he should have . . .

Maybe all this time he'd been wrong. Maybe all this time Frankie had been hiding her attraction to him the same way he'd hidden his attraction to her.

The thought nearly made his head explode. He knew he was looking at Frankie with pure hunger in his eyes, but he couldn't stop himself.

"If we don't get back to work, this is going to take all night," Frankie said, trying hard to be businesslike.

"I've got all night."

Simon's words were loaded with meaning, and Frankie had to turn away, afraid of letting him see the look she knew was on her face.

Simon Hunt wasn't indifferent to her after all. The news filled her with a wide variety of sensations. Pleasure. Excitement. Delight. Panic.

Particularly panic.

She felt oddly like the creator of some horrible monster, knowing that if she glanced back at Simon again, he'd still be gazing at her with that fiercely burning heat in his eyes. She'd seen him look at women like that before—other women, never her. Until now.

Jazz. What happened to the excitement she'd been feeling about seeing Jazz again? It was nothing. It was buried underneath the knowledge that with little effort, sophisticated and incredibly sexy Simon Hunt could very well share her bed in the very near future.

And tomorrow Frankie would wake up to find the nearly twenty-year friendship she had with this man destroyed. Tomorrow she'd wake up and join the ranks of women like Maia Fox. She'd join the legion of women whom Simon had loved and left. And she used the word *loved* only in the very loosest physical sense.

At least she wouldn't make the mistake of believing that she could change Simon. At least she wouldn't be foolish enough to hope that he would treat her any differently from the hordes of foolish women who had come before her.

She wouldn't do that—because she wasn't going to sleep with Simon. Not tonight. Not ever. Provided he didn't catch her at a particularly weak moment. Provided she didn't get pulled in by the molten lava of his gaze.

"Just get back to work," she told him, carefully keeping her eyes on the copy machine.

FOUR

"Figured I'd find you girl-watching," Leila Hunt said, slipping into the seat across from Simon's at the resort restaurant. "Good grief, is that *Frankie*?"

Simon nodded.

"What is she wearing? Is she wearing . . . ?"

"A dress."

"Who's she with? He's not bad. Really nice smile—"

"He's a client." Simon's words came out a little too tight, a little too clipped, and his sister looked at him in surprise.

"Of yours?"

Simon forced himself to relax, to smile, to hide the fact that he was sitting there with his insides tied in knots because Francine Paresky was sitting all the way across the room, actually wearing one of the dresses—the blue-flowered one—he'd found in her closet, and having dinner with Clayton Quinn.

That could have been him sitting there. It should have been.

"No, believe it or not, the client's hers," he told Leila, and his voice actually sounded natural. He sounded lighthearted and even slightly disinterested. "She's working on a case for this guy, trying to locate the beneficiary to a will."

"That's great." Leila took a bread stick from the basket in the center of the table, breaking off a piece and popping it into her mouth. "Just yesterday Frankie was telling me she was so broke, she was going to have to go back to chartering fishing trips here at the resort for Preston Seaholm."

"Oh, man, you're kidding." Simon grimaced, pulling his gaze away from the animated conversation Frankie was having with Clay Quinn to look at his sister. "I thought she swore she'd never do that again."

Leila's violet eyes were dead serious. "Taxes are coming due. She didn't have much of a choice."

Two years earlier Frankie had worked regularly at the resort, taking groups of vacationers on expeditions on Pres Seaholm's fishing boat. The groups were usually all men, and they usually drank quite a bit of beer as they fished. Sometimes the guests got rowdy and very rude. Once Frankie had felt sufficiently threatened to dump her life-vest-clad passengers into the ocean and haul them back to the harbor by ropes tossed off the stern.

Simon never found out exactly what happened to set off that chain of events, but Leila had hinted that several of the guests decided that the money they were paying Frankie to captain the charter boat entitled them to certain sexual favors.

Yes, Frankie had been able to take care of herself, but Simon shuddered to think what might have happened if those men had been a little more inebriated, or a little more determined to have their way.

Frankie was tough, but she was barely five feet. A six-foot-tall man would be able to overpower her rather easily. And she wouldn't stand a fighting chance against a group of men.

Man, just the thought of her working that charter boat again made Simon's heart lodge in his throat. But she wasn't going to have to do that, he told himself. She had this investigation job for Clay Quinn. Thank God for Quinn.

"I got a call from Mom today," Leila told him. "She's going to stay with her friends on St. John for another month. She's actually thinking about buying a condo down there."

"Uh-huh," Simon said absently, not really paying attention to his sister. He was staring across the restaurant again, watching as Frankie laughed at something Quinn said. Damn Quinn anyway. Damn him for sitting where Simon ought to be sitting.

Frankie's eyes were sparkling and she was smiling, her dark hair gleaming in the restaurant's dim lighting. Simon quickly pulled his own eyes away from her, well aware that Leila was watching him.

His face had been expressionless—he knew it had been. But Leila was looking at him, her eyes slightly narrowed. "Si, are you . . . ?" She couldn't possibly have seen anything on his face, but still, somehow she knew. "My God, you *are*."

She was guessing. She couldn't possibly know for certain what he was thinking and feeling. No way. "I'm what?" he asked, his voice cool and calm.

Leila was blunt. "You're targeting my best friend to be your next flavor of the week."

Simon made himself laugh. "Don't be ridiculous."

"It *does* sound ridiculous, doesn't it? I say the words, and they sound utterly ridiculous. You and *Frankie* . . . ?"

Simon took a careful sip of his drink. The soda was cold, and the rum felt warm. Together they made his stomach jump. What was wrong with him? "Obviously your imagination is on overload."

"But I saw you staring at Frankie with that look in your eyes," Leila said.

"*What* look?"

"*You* know the look I mean. The one where you *really* look."

"Of course I'm *really* looking. I'm curious. I've never seen Francine wear a dress before. It's bizarre."

Leila didn't believe his protests for one second. She laughed, looking at her brother with both pity and amusement in her eyes. "She will never—never in a million years—fall for your lines. She's seen you in action way too many times for that to happen."

"For what to happen?"

Leila looked up as her fiancé and Simon's longtime friend, Marsh Devlin, pulled a chair up to the table and sat down. The way she instantly transformed was amazing. Simon's sister was quite attractive with her violet eyes, short blond curls, and sweetly heart-shaped face. Still, she was nothing truly exceptional. But when she looked at Marshall Devlin, her love for the man became an almost tangible, visible thing and she became incredibly, breathtakingly gorgeous.

And Dev. Dev had been his best friend for years, and Simon had never seen him look so thoroughly happy.

He couldn't help but feel a pang of envy. He'd been avoiding Dev and Leila lately, he realized. The pair still disagreed and had spirited debates—they probably always would. But they clearly loved each other. Their love and happiness made them seem so . . . complete. Every time Simon was with them, he felt like a puzzle with several pieces missing.

"What are you doing here?" he asked them. "Celebrating your ten-and-half-week engagement anniversary or something?"

Marsh smiled across the table at Leila, and Simon had to stifle his annoyance. They deserved to be happy. He, on the other hand, deserved nothing. He glanced at Frankie again. And nothing was exactly what he was getting.

"Actually we're meeting Jesse here for dinner," Marsh told Simon in his crisp English accent.

Simon sat up. "Jesse's in town?" Marsh's American half brother was nearly ten years their junior. It had been years since Simon had last seen Jesse Devlin. He remembered him as a tall, athletic college kid more interested in baseball than in school and grades. He had to be . . . what? Twenty-seven years old now—not a kid anymore.

"I think he's here to try to borrow some money," Marsh said with a rueful grin. "He doesn't believe a doctor could be anything but loaded. We'll have to set him straight." He took in Simon's well-groomed hair and casually dressy clothes. "You're not here alone, are you? You could join us—"

"Simon's got a thing for Frankie," Leila announced, and Marsh's smile turned to a look of astonishment.

"Frankie Paresky?"

"Fine." Simon spread his hands as if he didn't give a damn what Leila said or Marsh believed. "Spread rumors about your best friend."

"He was sitting here, looking at her," Leila told Marsh. "You know the way I mean. He was looking at her as if he were wishing she was something he could order from the menu."

"So I was watching her." Simon heard exasperation creep into his voice. "She looks really good tonight. So I find her attractive. I find all women attractive."

"No, you don't."

"Yes, I do. It's no big deal."

"I know how you operate—"

"I should have gone someplace else—"

"It starts with a crush, an *attraction*—"

"But my *date* wanted to come here," Simon finished.

As if on cue, the woman he'd met an hour earlier out on the resort patio swept into the restaurant.

She was a knockout. She was wearing a skin-tight pale pink dress that accentuated her hourglass figure. The dress was outrageously short, and her legs were long and shapely. Her hair was red, and pulled up off her neck in a haphazard fashion that made her look both seductive and innocent.

"Your date?" Leila repeated with a frown.

"Here she is." Simon knew his sister's theory about why he was watching Frankie was shot to hell, and he smiled his triumph. He stood up. "Say hi to Jesse for me."

He could feel Leila and Marsh watching him as he crossed the room toward—he couldn't remember his date's name. Damn. He felt a flash of panic. What was wrong with him? He never forgot a name, let alone the name of a beautiful woman.

Chloe. That was it. Thank God.

As he offered Chloe his arm, Simon felt yet another pair of eyes upon him. He turned, and sure enough Frankie was watching him, but she quickly looked away.

What had gone wrong?

He'd spent most of the afternoon with Frankie down in the real estate office's basement, searching through files and records. At one point he'd been virtually certain that he and Francine Paresky were going to end up in bed together. Tonight. The thought was dizzyingly, heart-poundingly exciting. Frankie in his bed, in his arms.

For months it had seemed as if his libido were out to lunch, but suddenly, just like that, his body was back on-line, ready to go. *Really* ready to go . . .

So what had happened? They'd finished copying and highlighting the rental records. Frankie had flipped through them all but there were too many and it was too late to examine them completely.

Simon had suggested going out for pizza and Frankie had hesitated just a fraction of a second before accepting.

It was that—that little bit of hesitation—that made Simon realize this was no flirtatious game. This was real life. Frankie was his friend, not some stranger he could have a brief, passionate affair with.

She'd practically grown up in his house—the entire Hunt clan taking warmly to the little girl with the southern drawl who lived in a tiny house with her gram. She'd had no parents. Her mom had died and her dad had split. Simon's own mother and father, while not exactly June and Ward Cleaver but damn close, had included Frankie in nearly every family outing. She'd always been around. Simon had assumed she always would be around.

Unless he did something to drive her away.

He couldn't play this game. The stakes were too high.

Of course he was assuming Frankie would even allow herself to be seduced. Just because she hesitated before accepting his dinner invitation didn't mean anything.

He was reading far too much into it. Three seconds of hesitation didn't necessarily mean that she took the time to imagine going home with him after dinner. It didn't mean that during those few seconds she'd delayed, she'd imagined the two of them, *sans* clothing, locked together in a steamy embrace.

It was possible that her hesitation wasn't the result of any extra thought. It was entirely possible that she hadn't spoken right up because she'd burped.

Besides, it wasn't even dinner—it was pizza, for crying out loud.

Still, he wasn't sure which he was more afraid of, that Frankie would reject him or that she'd allow herself to be seduced and ruin their friendship. And he didn't trust himself enough to take her to dinner and then take her home. He knew himself well enough to know he'd finagle an invitation inside and then he'd be facing either rejection or disaster.

So he'd rescinded his invitation. He'd made some lame excuse about how he'd just remembered a previous engagement. He'd told her he'd see her in the morning at the house on Pelican Street, and he'd gotten the hell out of there.

He'd gone home and showered and changed and headed for the resort. That was when he met Chloe. She'd been wearing a gauzy beach cover-up over a microscopic bikini that was a polar opposite to the bathing suit Frankie had been wearing earlier that day. Chloe had accepted his dinner invitation immediately, boldly inviting him up to her suite while she showered and changed.

He'd declined.

What was wrong with him? He'd asked Chloe to dinner with the express intention of going back to her room with her tonight. It was an attempt to substitute a more experienced player into the game he'd started with Frankie. It was an attempt to curb this incredible sense of restlessness that was surely caused by sexual need.

But it wasn't working—at least not the way he'd planned.

Because despite her sexy dress and make-it-with-me shoes, Chloe left him cold.

"Simon, isn't it?" Clay Quinn said with a smile, raising his voice to be heard over the dance band that had begun playing in the corner of the room. "Nice to see you again."

Frankie turned around to find Simon standing behind her.

He was dressed in the island's version of semi-formal—lightweight ivory pants and a pastel-green polo shirt, sandals on his feet. The colors went well with his thick blond hair and his tropical tan. He looked good. *Too* good. Frankie forced her eyes back to her plate.

"I didn't expect to run into you here." Simon's words were addressed to her.

She braced herself before she glanced back up at him. "I called Clay to say that I'd remembered Jazz's last name—it's Chester—and he invited me to join him for a bite to eat."

"Have a seat." Clay moved the small pad of hotel stationery he'd been jotting notes on, making room at the table for Simon. "Join us."

"Actually," Simon said, "I was hoping to steal my boss for just a moment, if I may."

"Of course."

His boss? It took Frankie a moment to realize he was talking about *her*.

Simon took her hand and drew her out of her seat.

"Simon, what are you doing?" He was leading her onto the wooden dance floor.

"This is called dancing, Francine. Think you can manage to do it without standing in a line and wearing cowboy boots?"

Frankie didn't want to be there. She didn't want to be clasped in Simon Hunt's arms, his body dangerously close to hers, moving slowly in time to the strains of an old romantic song.

"I don't want to dance."

"Humor me," Simon said. "I'm messing with my sister's mind."

"By dancing with *me*?"

"Yeah."

"Whatever this is about, I don't want to know, do I?"

"Probably not," Simon said.

"But I definitely don't want to dance with you. Whatever trick you're playing on Leila, you can do it without my help." Frankie tried to break out of his grasp.

But he didn't let her go. "If you don't dance with

me, I won't tell you the brilliant solution I've come up with to find Jazz Chester."

Simon was a graceful dancer, moving with a smooth confidence that told of years of experience. Frankie remembered how she and Leila had giggled when he had signed up for a ballroom-dancing class at the senior center one summer when he was home from college. He'd learned to dance *and* charmed his way into the hearts of many of the island's wealthy older residents, most of whom became the foundation of his antiques business's client list.

On the rare occasions that Frankie had danced with Simon in the past, she'd closed her eyes and allowed herself to relax. She'd let herself fantasize a perfect world—one in which Simon Hunt would change. He wouldn't change a great deal. He'd still be sharp-witted and confident. He'd still ooze sexiness and charm, and have that aura of danger, that heartbreaker's attitude. He'd even still break hearts—everyone's but hers. When it came to Frankie, though, he'd be radically different. He'd personify the word *fidelity*. He'd become the poster model for true, everlasting love.

Talk about fantasies . . .

Tonight Frankie couldn't muster up the energy to fantasize. Not with the woman in the pink minidress—clearly the previous engagement Simon had suddenly remembered at the real estate office—standing next to the bar. The facts canceled out the fantasy, and the fact was, Simon was going home with this other woman tonight. Lord help her, but Frankie didn't want to think about that.

"I had a great idea, but I didn't want to make any promises in front of Clay," Simon told Frankie. "Tell me if I'm remembering correctly. Didn't you say your buddy Jazz went to Boston University?"

Frankie nodded, allowing herself only the briefest glance up into his eyes. Great idea or not, she hated that he was dancing with her. She hated knowing that later he was going to dance with Miss Pink over there and compare and contrast his two dance partners. Or maybe he wouldn't bother to compare them at all. Maybe Miss Pink had no comparison. Maybe Simon didn't even consider Frankie to be the same *species* as the willowy redhead.

"I have a friend who works at B.U.'s alumni office," Simon continued. "He owes me a favor. If you want, I can call and ask him to search the computers for Jazz Chester's most recent address."

Frankie forgot about the redhead. She forgot that she was dancing. She forgot *everything*, including the danger of gazing for any length of time into Simon's blue eyes. "Are you serious?" she said, staring up at him. It *was* a great idea.

"Absolutely."

He was incredibly handsome, with laugh lines crinkling around his eyes, with his perfect white teeth and slightly crooked smile. His eyes were an almost unearthly turquoise shade of blue, interrupted by tiny flecks of gold and green.

His smile warmed his eyes as he gazed down at

her, and then suddenly, subtly, something changed. The warmth became heat and his friendly gaze became an almost palpable caress moving across her face.

Frankie stopped breathing. She couldn't move, couldn't resist as Simon gently drew her in so that her body was pressed fully, intimately, against his.

He lowered his head, and she knew without a doubt that he was going to kiss her. But he didn't. He stopped, his lips mere inches from hers, and for the first time in Frankie's life she saw doubt and a strange sort of uncertainty in Simon Hunt's eyes.

She didn't have a clue as to what he saw in *her* eyes, but whatever it was—probably pure panic—it made him pull away from her.

The song ended as Simon continued to back off, putting distance between them.

"I'll call my friend at Boston University first thing in the morning."

Frankie nodded. What just happened? "Thanks."

"I guess I'll, um . . . I'll see you. Tomorrow morning."

He walked her back to her table and nodded his thanks to Clay Quinn. He barely met her eyes one last time before he vanished into the crowd.

Simon was embarrassed. Frankie wished she knew why. Was it because he'd momentarily dropped his guard and allowed her to see past the confidence in his eyes? Or was it because he'd almost kissed her?

Lord, was the idea of kissing her really that embarrassing?

◆――――――◆

"Interested in coming up to my room for a night-cap?"

Simon gazed across the table at Chloe's movie-star-perfect face. She was gorgeous. Everything about her was amazing—from her elegant features to her perfectly proportioned curves. And she was inviting him to her room.

Her eyes told him this was not to be taken lightly. Not everyone she dated was issued this kind of invitation.

He knew she liked him. He'd kept her amused all throughout dinner. And the way her eyes skimmed over his body gave him the not-so-subtle hint that she found him physically attractive too.

Simon knew he could go back to her room with her, and inside fifteen minutes, tops, he'd be in her bed. Having sex. With her.

Casual, no-strings sex with a beautiful stranger. It was all a man with his reputation could possibly want.

Except he didn't want it.

He honest-to-God didn't want *her*.

He thought his napping libido had finally awakened for good that afternoon while he was in the real estate office. And again, while he was dancing with Frankie, he'd felt the unmistakable rush of sexual attraction. Lust. The sensation was as familiar to him as breathing.

But as Simon sat down to dinner with Chloe, Frankie had finished her coffee, and she and Clay

Quinn had left the restaurant. Simon watched as they parted ways in the lobby, Clay heading toward his room and Frankie toward the door to the parking lot. And as Frankie left, his desire had vanished too.

Chloe was nice to look at, but she was lacking just a bit when it came to imagination and opinions. In fact, it seemed to Simon as if she had none of either.

All night long he'd been fighting the urge to look at his watch. All night long he'd been waiting for the right moment to make his escape.

What he couldn't figure out was why. Why not go to Chloe's room and engage in a little one-on-one? Why the hell *not*?

He forced himself to look at the woman sitting across from him, *really* look at her. She was incredible. She had large, full breasts and a narrow waist, a flat stomach and mind-blowingly long legs. So she wasn't a Rhodes scholar. So what?

Two years ago he wouldn't have turned her down. Why was he turning her down now? And he was. He was going to turn her down the same way he'd turned down similar invitations, going on four months now.

Four months. He'd actually been celibate for four *months*.

Four months without sex, and now he was being handed an opportunity to end his dry streak with a woman who looked like a Playboy bunny, and he still wasn't interested. He felt nothing for her. No sexual pull, no chemistry, no attraction, no nothing. *Nothing*. It was weird, but true.

Like all the women he'd dated over the past four

months, he had absolutely no desire to get past a superficial first-date-type relationship with Chloe. And sex seemed far too intimate an activity to share with someone he didn't even want to talk to anymore.

"Thanks," Simon said, "but I'd better get on home. I've got to be up early in the morning."

Chloe thought he was nuts, and he had to agree. He was definitely insane. But moments later he was in the parking lot, unlocking the door of his sports car, relieved to finally be on his way home.

As he opened the driver's side door, he saw a car pull out of the lot, a car that looked like Frankie's little import. He turned, trying to get a closer look or a glimpse of the driver.

It wasn't Frankie.

It wasn't *Frankie*.

The realization hit him so hard, he had to sit down. He slid behind the steering wheel and gripped it tightly. He hadn't gone up to Chloe's room because she *wasn't Frankie*. If Frankie Paresky had put forth the same proposition to him, he would not have turned her down. He would have been up in her room so fast . . . Damn, they wouldn't even have made it up to her room. Simon would've hit the stop button and made love to her right there in the elevator.

The thought was sobering and a tad alarming. And exciting as hell. Simon closed his eyes, imagining himself with Frankie in a stopped elevator, clothes askew, surrounded by four walls of mirrors, Frankie's legs wrapped around his waist, her head thrown back in pleasure as he buried himself inside her again and again and again. . . .

Sweet Lord, he'd had Frankie in his arms tonight. He'd been that close, *that* close to kissing her, but he'd chickened out. He'd gotten a sudden strange case of nerves. What if he kissed her and she laughed at him? What if he kissed her and she gave him a classic rejection speech about how they should just be friends? What if . . .

That was crazy. *He* was crazy. So what if she laughed at him? He'd just kiss her until she stopped laughing. And she *would* stop laughing.

To hell with twenty years of friendship. To hell with potential disaster. To hell with it all. Whatever happened, it would be worth even just one sweet moment of passion. He wanted her so badly, he would gladly trade all twenty years for one single incredible night.

Simon started his car with a roar.

Next time he wouldn't chicken out.

FIVE

Simon looked like hell.

He climbed out of his little black sports car looking as if he hadn't slept all night.

He probably hadn't.

Frankie leaned against the railing at number six Pelican Street, trying not to hate the woman Simon had no doubt spent the night with, trying to convince herself that she didn't care.

But she *did* care. She'd gone to sleep the night before thinking about finding Jazz Chester, yet it was Simon Hunt who'd haunted her dreams.

No more, she silently vowed, turning her attention to Clay Quinn, who was struggling to unlock the big wooden door. From then on she was going to concentrate her efforts—waking *and* sleeping—on finding Jazz.

Clay's cellular phone trilled, and he gave up on the

door for a moment as he answered it, moving to the far side of the porch.

"Morning." Simon's voice was husky, and Frankie knew if she turned around, he'd be standing much too close.

Still, she couldn't resist. She turned around.

He was wearing dark glasses and his hair was still damp from what had no doubt been a hurried shower. Despite the heat, he carried a mug bearing the logo of the doughnut shop on the corner of Ocean and Main, and sipped hot coffee through a slot in the plastic lid. He wore plaid Bermuda shorts with a white polo shirt, boat shoes on his feet, and no socks. His legs were muscular and tan and covered with golden-tinted hair that gleamed in the sunshine.

He looked much too good despite the fact that he was clearly exhausted. He smiled at her. "Hey."

"Hey." Frankie backed away, putting more space between them.

"I have some good news and some bad news," Simon said. "Which do you want first?"

Clay closed up his phone and went back to wrestling with the door. "Sorry about that," he called out. "The office is going crazy—one of our longtime clients was arrested last night. I've been getting constant phone calls since five-thirty this morning." His phone rang again. "Damn!"

He kept working on the door, opening his phone and sticking it under his chin. Frankie turned back to Simon. "I want only good news," she told him. "As far as I'm concerned, you can just skip anything bad."

"I called my friend at Boston University." Simon lowered his voice and Frankie was forced to step closer to hear him. "He said it's illegal to give out an alumnus's personal information, but when I explained what we needed the address for, he said he'd make an exception."

"That's great," Frankie said. "So what's the bad news?"

As Clay Quinn muscled the front door open, still talking on his phone, Simon took off his sunglasses and put them in his pocket. His eyes didn't look tired or slightly bloodshot as she'd imagined. They were clear and bright. She had to look away.

"I thought you didn't want the bad news," Simon countered, following her into the house.

Clay went directly toward the back, toward the kitchen, as he continued to talk on his cellular phone. His voice echoed eerily in the stillness.

It was dark inside. And cool. The air conditioner was still in working order. It had chugged away for eight years, with only old Axel Bayard coming by periodically to give it a tune-up. Frankie stood for a moment in the foyer, letting her eyes adjust. She remembered this house. Alice Winfield had always kept the curtains open wide, letting the bright Florida sunshine in. Every surface had been scrubbed clean, every window gleamed. The old woman would have clucked her tongue at the years of dust and neglect.

"I was lying," Frankie said. "Tell me the bad news."

"My friend wasn't at the office. He was home."

Simon went into the front parlor and pulled open the heavy draperies. Sunlight streamed weakly through the grimy windows, illuminating the dust that hung heavily in the air. "He's got the flu. He won't be back at work until Thursday—at the earliest."

"Oh, *shoot*." Thursday. Today was Tuesday. Two whole days of *waiting* . . .

"He also told me there was no guarantee that the information he had would be up-to-date," Simon continued. The furniture in the room was covered by ghostly-looking white sheets. He lifted one and looked beneath it, then whisked it off. "Oh, man, would you look at this!"

Frankie looked. It was a boxy-looking sideboard-type table made of dark, grainy wood.

"Oak," Simon said, awe in his voice. "That's oak. It's a Stickley piece. This thing must weigh a *ton*." He took a tiny penlight from his pocket and scrambled onto the floor, on his back, sticking his arm and as much of his head as he could underneath the table.

"Yes!" he exclaimed. "A red seal! This is *great*!"

"A red what . . . ?"

"The older, more valuable pieces were built by Gustav Stickley," Simon told her, pulling himself up off the floor, ignoring the dust that covered him. "They all had a label—a red seal that identified 'em. The later pieces had a black seal. They aren't as valuable."

He moved to pull another sheet off a hidden piece of furniture, but stopped, glancing up at Clay Quinn, who stood in the doorway, holstering his phone. "Do you mind?" he asked.

Quinn shrugged. "Not if you cover it up again when you're done."

Frankie watched as Simon went quickly around the room. He pulled all the coverings off furniture made with that same dark wood in that same straight style and turned them over or looked underneath the pieces.

"It's *all* red-seal Stickley," Simon said. "It's in perfect condition too."

Clay's phone rang again, and he vanished in the direction of the kitchen. Simon tossed Frankie the pile of sheets as he raced into the dining room, eager to see what other treasures lay within.

Frankie put the sheets down on the back of a Victorian-era sofa. She'd shared many a glass of iced tea with Alice Winfield, right in this very room, sitting on this very sofa.

The parlor had been Alice's favorite room. It had a big bay window that looked out over the ocean. Together they'd munched homemade cookies and Alice would talk about her years teaching in a small town near Midland, Michigan. She'd actually taught in a one-room schoolhouse, and as a young girl Frankie had been fascinated by those stories.

Over in the corner was Alice's rolltop desk. Frankie pulled out the chair and pushed up the top. Everything was neatly arranged in the cubbyholes, just as Alice had left it. Blank stationery and envelopes were in one slot. A roll of Scotch tape and a tiny tin of rubber cement were in another. A small accounts book was in a third. Frankie took it out and opened it up.

Alice's handwriting was angular and familiar. She'd kept careful track of the money she'd spent on food and clothing while she was on Sunrise Key. Another page was devoted to telephone, electric, and gas bills.

There was no mention of neighbors, no personal information.

The desk drawers were filled with neatly stacked blank paper and other office supplies. Pens. Pencils. Rubber bands. Scissors. A small box filled with time-hardened erasers of all shapes and sizes. Twelve-cent postage stamps. Several neatly rubber-banded decks of playing cards.

Frankie closed the desk and crossed to the bookshelf where Alice had kept her photo albums. Frankie had loved to pull them down and look at the seemingly ancient photographs of old-fashioned people in their outdated clothing. It was a window to the past. She loved the picture of a young, laughing Alice, her face wrinkle free as she stood arm in arm with her handsome husband.

Alice kept the photo albums in chronological order on the shelf, always adding a new one every three or four years or so. Frankie found the latest and pulled it free. The top was covered with dust and she carefully wiped it clean as she carried it to the sofa. She set it on her lap as she sat down and opened it.

Alice, standing outside, next to her garden. Frankie had taken that picture. Alice's face may not have been smooth, but her smile was still young and her eyes sparkled with girlish pleasure.

Frankie flipped back a few pages, and there, carefully glued to the black paper of the book, was a photograph of Alice, Frankie, and Jazz.

Jazz's stepfather—the man Frankie believed was the mysterious John—had taken the photo.

Dear Lord, Frankie had been so young back then. She'd been barely eighteen, and the world had seemed so full of promise. Her future had seemed so crystal-clear. Jazz had said he loved her, and she had no reason to believe that their love wouldn't last until the end of time—until they both were even older and wiser than Alice Winfield.

Boy, had she been wrong. Jazz had left Sunrise Key, never to return. Alice Winfield had disappeared some years later, kept by her poor health from ever again returning to her beloved house on Sunrise Key. Frankie's eyes filled with tears.

Eight years. Alice had been alive for eight years, and nobody had bothered to tell Frankie.

She would have written. She would have sent pictures of the ocean and the sky. She would have come to this house and done battle with the dirt and dust. She even would have traveled up to Michigan to visit the old woman.

She turned the page to a picture of Alice standing at the gas grill on the back porch, waving at the camera—waving at Frankie, who had taken the picture, and her tears overflowed.

Alice had probably thought Frankie hadn't cared.

"Hey, Frankie, are you okay?"

Simon sat down on the sofa next to her, his eyes dark with concern.

She hastily tried to wipe her face, but the tears wouldn't stop. She swore, closing the photo album, afraid of getting it wet, afraid of Simon's gentle pity. "I'm fine."

He knew she wasn't. He reached out, gently touching the back of her head, softly stroking her hair. His hand was warm, and when she glanced up at him, his eyes were soft.

"I'm not fine," she admitted. "Alice Winfield was special to me."

Simon nodded. There was nothing mocking in his gaze, nothing but gentleness in his slight smile. "That's what I like about you, Francine," he said quietly. "You know every single person who lives on this island—and everyone who's ever lived on this island. And to you, every single one of them is special in some way."

He glanced away from her, out the dirt-streaked windows at the brilliant blue of the sky. "Alice Winfield was no angel. She was outspoken and blunt to the point of rudeness. She was also pretty damn miserly. But you focused on her good side."

"She was *careful* with her money. When she was growing up—"

Simon cut her off with a smile. "Hey, I'm not attacking her." He shifted toward her on the couch, reaching out to touch her hair again. "I'm just marveling at the way you can overlook the negative and always find some redeeming quality in just about anyone."

Frankie had to look away. The sensation of his fingers in her hair and the quiet warmth in his eyes was damn near overwhelming. But she couldn't pull away. She closed her eyes, allowing herself to enjoy the gentleness of his touch.

"How about me, Francine," Simon said softly. "What do you see when you look at me?"

He was leaning in, closer to her, his breath warm against her ear. If she turned her head, his lips would be a whisper away from hers. If she turned her head, he would kiss her, and Frankie knew without a shadow of a doubt that that single kiss would lead to much more.

What did she see?

Suddenly, with extreme clarity, Frankie saw a vision of the woman in the pink dress, the woman Simon had spent the night with. It had probably been only hours since he'd left her bed. Apparently, now that Simon had gotten his "previous commitment" taken care of, he felt he could concentrate once more on Frankie.

Frankie stood up. "I see someone who's been my friend for a long time," she told him as she crossed to the big bay window. "Someone who's about to make a really bad mistake."

"It might be a mistake, but I'm not sure it's such a bad one."

She turned to face him. "It is. Absolutely."

He didn't move. He just gazed into her eyes as if

he were looking for answers, searching for hidden truths. "How can you be so positive?"

Frankie wasn't positive. She wasn't positive about *any*thing when it came to Simon Hunt. Especially when he looked at her that way. But she steadily returned his gaze, and without a tremor in her voice she said, "Si, I'm on the verge of finding Jazz Chester again, and I feel like this could be a real important milestone in my life." She was trying as much to convince herself as she was to convince him.

"What if he's not as great as you remember him to be?"

"What if he's better?"

Simon was still watching her intently, and Frankie forced herself to stare back at him. He didn't quite believe her, and rightfully so. But what was she supposed to tell him? That she couldn't risk acting on this sexual attraction that had suddenly ignited between them? That she couldn't risk giving in to the temptations that her body desired because it wouldn't take much for her heart to become involved?

Shoot, her heart already *was* involved. When she daydreamed about Simon, she wasn't dreaming about a sexy bed partner. She was dreaming about a *lover*. And that was where fantasy and reality became hopelessly entangled. She dreamed about someone who did more than fulfill her passionate physical fantasies, someone who satisfied her emotional needs as well. Someone who used sexual intimacy as a means to express his deepest feelings of love rather than someone—like Simon—who played at love to achieve sexual gratification.

Frankie could pretend to be a willing participant in the kind of casual, no-strings relationship that Simon was so good at having. She knew she would enjoy the physical intimacies she saw promised in the heat of his eyes. In fact, a good part of her was tempted . . .

Jazz, she reminded herself. It was only a matter of time before she found Jazz Chester again. Compared to Jazz's deep sensitivity, Simon would seem frivolous and shallow.

"Alice liked Jazz too," she told Simon. "She was so certain that we were going to end up together, you know, get married. When Jazz didn't come back to Sunrise Key, Alice was almost as upset as I was. She told me that she wished she could wave a magic wand and make him appear. She said she'd do *any*thing to get the two of us back together. She didn't manage to do it while she was alive, but she just might be able to pull it off now that she's gone." Simon finally looked away, and Frankie knew that she had won—this round at least.

And she herself was starting to believe her own words. Finding Jazz was going to be good.

Simon glanced up at Frankie again as she moved toward the bookcase and slipped the photo album onto the shelf. Damn Jazz Chester. He'd disliked what little he'd known about the boy, and those feelings held true for the man.

Simon had seldom had rivals when it came to a woman's affections. This jealousy he was trying hard to curb was an uncomfortable sensation. He didn't like knowing that he couldn't even compete with a man that Frankie hadn't seen for twelve years.

But that didn't mean Simon was going to give up.

"I think you're holding out for a dream," he told her. Even if Jazz *weren't* married, he couldn't possibly be as perfect as Frankie remembered. No way. The flowers and poetry had to be part of some cheeseball act designed to make it easier to worm his way onto a young girl's beach blanket.

She glanced at him, her dark eyes unreadable and finally dry. Man, when he'd come back into the parlor to find her crying, his insides had twisted, and all thoughts about the incredible antique treasures he'd found throughout the entire house had fled.

"So what if I am?"

So what, indeed? Jazz *was* going to be a disappointment, and Simon was going to be there to pick up the pieces.

Frankie finished her perusal of the bookcase and headed out of the room toward the stairs leading to the second floor of the house. Simon trailed after her.

Clay Quinn was still on the telephone, his voice muffled behind the closed kitchen door.

"What's the furniture like in the dining room?" Frankie asked, climbing the stairs, pointedly changing the subject.

"Perfect. It's all red-seal Stickley oak too. In fact, I've been searching for a dining room set just like it. I have a client who has an end-of-the-month deadline, and if I don't come up with something, he's going to go with inferior pieces from another broker."

She glanced at him over her shoulder. "Isn't the end of the month—"

"Next Monday. We need to find this John guy before next Monday, or you don't get your bonus and I don't make this deal."

Simon followed Frankie into a room that must have been Alice Winfield's bedroom. The heavy curtains were drawn and the room was only dimly lit by the light from the hall.

"I don't think we should count on my friend at Boston University coming through with a current address for Jazz," Simon continued. "I think we need to go through those rental records we copied and try to find John's last name that way."

Frankie turned to face him, her delicate features mysterious in the gloom. "We?"

"Let me help you find this guy," he said.

She didn't say anything. She just looked at him.

"All private eyes have sidekicks," Simon continued. "Sherlock Holmes has Watson. Spenser has Hawk. Rockford has his dad. Inspector Clouseau has Kato. . . ."

She finally spoke. "You don't think I can find John on my own."

"No! That's not true! That's not what this is about at all," Simon hastily assured her.

"What *is* it about?"

"It's the old two-heads-are-better-than-one thing. My schedule is light for the next few days, and"—she was still watching him, her face damn near expression-less—"and I have to confess, Francine, I'm still hold-ing out hope that I'll be able to get you into bed with me."

She looked surprised for the briefest fraction of a second, and then she laughed. "Finally, something that rings with truth."

Simon lowered his voice, suddenly aware of the quiet dimness of the room, of the big antique bed in the corner, covered by a protective sheet. "Just think how incredible it could be."

Something shifted in her eyes, something that told Simon that she, too, had imagined the nuclear heat the two of them could generate. "You're probably right." She turned away from him and crossed to the windows, pushing aside the curtains. "But I can tell you right now, Si, it's not going to happen. So if that's your motivation for helping—"

Simon squinted slightly in the sudden brightness. "I'm having fun, Francine. That—and the thought of making a very important client happy—is my motiva-tion."

"I was serious about what I said before, about you and me being a bad mistake."

"I know. And you're probably right."

"I'm definitely right. No means no. And if you repeatedly overstep those bounds—"

"I won't. I promise."

"I'm really sorry," Clay Quinn said from the door-way, and Simon nearly jumped with surprise. "But the manure has hit the fan back at my office and I've got to go. I've called the airport, and my charter flight is ready to leave as soon as I can get there. You're welcome to stay here in the house as long as you like. I'll leave you the keys—they're still down in the door."

Frankie nodded.

"Oh, and I'll give you my brother's phone number, in case I can't be reached." From his pocket Clay took a little notepad with the Seaholm Resort logo on the front. He scribbled a name and phone number on a sheet of the linen-blend paper, then tore it out and handed it to Frankie.

She glanced at it, folded it, and pocketed it. "If you don't mind, I'll let Simon—my assistant—drive you to the airport."

Her assistant. She was going to let him help. Simon knew he was grinning like an idiot, but he couldn't seem to stop. Frankie met his eyes only briefly, but it was long enough to send him a silent message: If he came on too strong, he'd be outta there.

Okay. He could play by those rules.

"Have a good flight," Frankie said to Clay.

"Thanks. I'll be in touch."

"I'll be back," Simon told Frankie, following Quinn out the door.

SIX

"Here's another two-week rental for John Marshall."
Simon reached for his notebook computer and deftly
typed the information into the file they'd started.
"April 1974."

"Great." Frankie looked over his shoulder. "How
many names do we have now?"

"Fifteen Johns," Simon said. "Five of them have
now rented on Pelican Street two years in a row."

The photocopies of rental records that they'd
made were spread out across Frankie's kitchen table.

"Why couldn't his first name have been Percival?"
Frankie mused.

"Or Fenton."

She snickered. "Or Beauregard."

"Dudley."

"Or Oscar?" Frankie shook her head, her laughter
turning to frustration. "Anything but *John*. This is
taking forever."

It better not take forever. Simon was running out of time.

It had nothing to do with his client's end-of-the-month deadline, and everything to do with his willpower. He'd been sitting at this table with Frankie for nearly six hours, and his strength was being severely tested. He'd memorized every single freckle on her nose and cheeks, he'd studied the way she caught her lower lip between her teeth when she was concentrating, and he'd stopped himself from reaching out for her more times than he could count.

He needed to find this man John, so he could find John's stepson, Jazz, so Frankie could see for herself that the guy was not worth her time.

Whereas Simon was?

No. But the time Frankie spent with Simon—preferably in Simon's bed—was going to be so incredible, it wasn't going to matter. It was going to be worth it.

At least it would be to Simon. Somehow—he didn't know how or why it had happened—Frankie held the key that would unlock him from this damned self-imposed state of monkhood he'd recently found himself in. Somehow, out of all of the women in the world, Frankie was the one woman that he wanted, the one woman who could set him free.

It *was* going to happen. He had to believe that.

"I wish there were a way to narrow down the dates," Simon said. "Lots of people take vacations the same two or three weeks each year. Are you sure Jazz and his family didn't—"

"I'm positive," Frankie interrupted. "Sometimes he was here in April, and sometimes he came down in February or March. The last year he came down it was early May. I know because—" She broke off. "Oh, my God."

"What?"

She shuffled through the papers on the table, searching for the date. "It was May, and it was a month before I turned eighteen. I know because I reread what I wrote in my diary just last night."

Simon stared across the table at her. "Your diary?" Frankie kept a *diary*? She hardly seemed the type. "Since when did you keep a diary?"

"Since forever," Frankie said, not even looking up. "I still do—sometimes." She found the page she was looking for and quickly skimmed the contents. "Shoot."

"What?"

She pushed the paper in front of him. "No first names."

Simon glanced down the list. "Here's Marshall again." He frowned. "But it's a different address than the two previous records."

Frankie snatched the page back from him and skewered it to the corkboard on the wall with a green pushpin. Then she bolted out of the kitchen. The swinging door rocked on its hinges as he heard her rapid footsteps up the stairs.

Curious, Simon followed, standing and stretching for the first time in what seemed like hours. He took the stairs to the second floor of the little house at a more leisurely pace.

The sun was starting to set, and Frankie had turned the light on in her room. Simon stopped in the doorway, watching as she moved from bookcase to bookcase, pulling spiral notebooks of all shapes and sizes from her shelves and tossing them onto the bed.

There were about thirty-five notebooks already there, and she showed no sign of stopping.

"Diaries," she said in response to his unspoken question. "I've always kept diaries. All we need to do is search through these for any mention of Jazz, and we'll have the dates that he was here on the key. We can cross-reference those dates with the rental records and hopefully come up with his stepdad's last name."

She dumped another armload on top of the pile, then sat down, cross-legged, her back against the headboard.

"I know it looks like a lot," she said, "but in the front of each book I always wrote the year. We can ignore the ones that I wrote before I turned ten, before Jazz first came to the key, and after I turned eighteen."

Frankie flipped open a notebook, quickly checked the date, tossed it onto the floor, then did the same with the next one.

Simon couldn't believe it. Was Frankie actually going to let him read her diaries?

She wasn't kidding when she said she'd been writing them forever. The bed was covered with pages and pages of her deepest thoughts. And passions. And desires . . .

Simon sat down on the edge of her bed and picked up one of the slim, spiral-bound books. He opened to a page in the middle.

December 20th, he read silently. Frankie's handwriting was bold and messy, but not unreadable.

> God, it's dark up here in Vermont. And cold. I knew when I took this scholarship that there wouldn't be enough money to go home for the holidays, but after two years in a row, I'm tired of being alone, and knowing how much Gram misses me doesn't help. The snow that I found so amusing back in November falls relentlessly. It's beautiful, but I want to go home. Five more months, and then two more years . . .

College. Frankie had written this when she'd gone away to college, Simon realized. It had taken her nearly three years after high school to save enough for her college tuition, even with the scholarship she'd won. But she'd never finished, never gotten her degree. He vaguely remembered her grandmother having a stroke or something that required Frankie's full-time care. He flipped ahead several pages, knowing that there was no reason for him to continue looking in this notebook, but unable to stop himself.

February 4th. Gram is in the hospital. Heart attack. Doc West called the school. I'm on the plane home, flying into Fort Myers, scared to death. She can't die. I won't let her die. It's been years since I've prayed, but I'm praying now. I thought I'd forgotten how.

Charlie drove me to the airport.

Charlie? Who was Charlie?

He knows I'm not coming back, but he told me that's okay. He said after he finishes grad school, he'll come down to Sunrise Key and then we'll get married.

Simon felt a twinge of jealousy, then forced himself to be rational. This Charlie was someone Frankie had known *years* ago. Clearly, things hadn't worked out between them. Whatever Frankie had felt for this man was well in the past.

Simon read further.

I told him I didn't want to marry him, and he got mad, but then he got all mushy and suffocating. He figures I'm talking that way only on account of my being upset about Gram. He told me that if I needed anything, all I had to do was call him. He's two years younger than me, but he's a senior and a man and he clearly thinks that he's got one up on me in the brains department. But he's the one who's slightly addled. He actually *thinks* I want to be taken care of.

Simon had to smile. Charlie may have been about to graduate from college, but clearly, he had a little bit more to learn—about Frankie in particular.

I wish we didn't have to talk, Frankie's diary continued. *I wish we could spend all our time making love—*

The jealousy was back, sharp and stabbing, bigger than a twinge. Simon glanced up at Frankie. Her full attention was on sorting through the other notebooks, so he read further.

I wish we could spend all our time making love, lost in pure physical pleasure, surrounded only by need, separate from what should be and what ought to be. When we make love, for a moment he forgets about being so damn pompous, so steady and down-to-earth. I can pretend that he brings me flowers, and that he believes love is something wild and uncontrollable, something he didn't plan to feel, something that makes him burn and shake.

But I know the truth. He loves the sex. And he loves my southern accent and the color of my eyes and the shape of my face, but he doesn't truly love *me*. He thinks if he can get me to dress the way he does in those boring sweaters and chinos, I'll make a cute little wife. He thinks that our babies will be pretty. They would be pretty, that's no lie.

But when I fell in love with Charlie I fell in love with a fantasy. I think his blond hair and blue eyes reminded me of Sunrise Key. To be brutally honest, the truth is, Charlie's handsome face reminded me of Simon Hunt—

Simon looked up, startled as Frankie snatched the notebook from his hands, shutting it in the process.

"You're not supposed to read 'em!" She stared down at the notebook, flipping open the cover. "You're just supposed to check the date and either put 'em in this pile, or toss 'em onto the floor." Her cheeks flushed as she saw that the book he had been reading dated from her years at college. But she pretended not to be embarrassed as she tossed the notebook onto the floor.

Charlie reminded me of Simon Hunt. . . .

She glanced up at him. "Are you helping or not?"

I wish we could spend all our time making love, lost in pure physical pleasure, surrounded only by need, separate from what should be and what ought to be. . . .

Simon picked up another notebook, suddenly very aware that he was in Francine's bedroom, sitting on her bed. There was no place on earth he'd rather be. Now, if he could only figure out a way to get all these notebooks off the bed and Frankie into his arms . . . He leaned back, propping himself up on one elbow. "How come I never heard about Charlie?"

She didn't answer right away. "I don't know. It wasn't as if he were some kind of secret."

He flipped open the cover of the book he held,

glancing down at the date. This diary was from only a few years before. Was he mentioned in there? Did she ever write about him? What did she say? He *had* to look. . . .

"You wrote that Charlie reminded you of me," Simon said.

Frankie took another notebook. "Did I really?" Her voice was even, matter-of-fact, and she didn't look up. "I don't remember."

She was lying. Simon was willing to bet she remembered every single intimate thought she ever wrote in these diaries. She was doing her best to ignore him, so he took advantage and put the book he was holding in front of him on the bed and quickly opened it to the middle. He picked up another notebook and lifted the cover, pretending to check the date as he read Frankie's now-familiar bold handwriting from the open book.

> Work, work, and more work. One fishing trip after another. I pull into the dock, let the happy fishers off, pick up the next group. I'm up before dawn and don't get home until way after dark. Maybe sometime next week it'll rain, and I'll sleep all day long. Maybe sometime in the next century I'll actually get a date. . . .

Simon turned several pages, looking for his name. Ah-ha!

Saw Simon downtown. Leila's due in for a visit next

week. I can't wait to see her—it's been too long. . . . She went on to write about her long-standing friendship with Simon's sister. Not one more word about Simon. He turned toward the back of the notebook.

. . . *the* last time *I'll* ever *wear a two-piece bathing suit*, she'd written at the top of the page, the underlined words catching his eye.

I should have known. I should have kept my T-shirt on, but it was so damn hot. I should have just sweated. I should have known that bunch was going to be trouble, with all their rude comments and innuendos.

I was helping the skinny guy pull in a fish. I didn't even feel the knife blade as the fat guy cut the back strap of my bathing suit. But just like that I was half naked.

It happened so fast. It's all a jumble of noises, hoots of laughter, and shouting. My own shouting. A blur of sensations, streaks of movement, action caught in a strobe light, embedded forever in my memory, playing over and over and over. I want it to go away. Maybe if I write it down . . .

I let go of the fishing pole, try to cover myself. A splash—the pole and the skinny man go overboard. The fat man laughs loud, wheezy laughter. His eyes are red and watery from too much beer and sun. "Hey, Hank, that's one hell of a pair you caught!" Anger—I was furious. How dare you? Groping hands, squeezing, touching my body, the stink of alcohol on his breath, more laughter—they're all laughing. I kick out, miss my target, connect with his thigh, mad as hell, how dare you? How *dare* you?

Simon felt as if he were choking, knowing that he was reading the words Frankie had written mere hours after she'd been attacked. He knew without a doubt that this was the incident that had made her quit her job at the marina, the job she had chartering Preston Seaholm's fishing boat. He turned the page, no longer even pretending not to read the words written there.

I kick him again and he's mad too, rips off what's left of my bathing suit top, pushes me down hard. On the deck on my back, knock over a bait bucket. Awash with briny water, little fish jumping, flopping, just like me, skittering on my elbows, trying to get away.

He read what she had written, heard the fear now mixed in with the anger. His heart was in his throat. Dear God, had she been raped? Had she not even told Leila the truth about what had happened that awful day? Simon knew with a dreadful certainty that whatever had happened, the truth was written right there, in that notebook. All he had to do to find out was to keep reading.

This can't be happening. Can't be . . .
He's on top of me—

Frankie whisked her diary away from him. "Dammit, Simon, didn't you hear what I just said? Doesn't privacy mean *any*thing to you?"

Simon looked up into the hot brown of Frankie's eyes and saw her gaze falter at the expression on his face. He reached for the diary, needing to finish reading, needing to know what had really happened. She pulled it away from him, so he reached for her instead.

Her eyes were wide with shock, her mouth opened slightly, and Simon realized there were tears in his own eyes.

"God, Frankie!" He pulled her toward him, enveloping her in his arms, burying his face in the sweetness of her short dark hair.

He was shaking with anger and outrage and fear. How could something that awful have happened to her here on Sunrise Key? He had probably been sitting at his desk that day. He'd probably been looking out the window of his home office at the crystal blue of the ocean, talking on the phone, laughing and joking—while she was lying on her back on the deck of the fishing boat. It killed him that he'd never known. It killed him that she'd never sought comfort from him.

He was comforting her now, but it was much, much too late. He felt her arms go up, around him, and suddenly she was holding him, comforting *him*. She didn't know why, didn't *have* to know why. Her friendship was unconditional, it always had been. And, oh, man, she smelled so good, felt so right in his arms. . . . But even that couldn't overpower his need to know the truth.

"Simon, what on earth is the matter? You're shaking. . . ."

"You've got to let me finish reading that." Simon's voice sounded harsh and strained even to his own ears.

"Reading what? I can't believe something I wrote in my diary could make you so—"

"The rape." He tried to say it flatly, but his voice faltered.

He felt her stiffen, felt the tension suddenly appear in his shoulders and back. She swore, just once, under her breath, and pulled away from him. He let go, suddenly afraid to touch her, afraid to move.

"Figures you had to read that one," she said, and swore again. She was unable to hold his gaze, looking down at the book in her hands, at the notebooks that she'd tossed onto her throw rug, out the window at the deepening twilight, looking anywhere but into his eyes.

"Why didn't you ever tell me?"

"I couldn't. I could hardly tell anyone."

"Not even Leila?"

She glanced up at him then, her expression guarded. She carefully closed the notebook. "I told Leila."

"Everything?"

A slight hesitation, but then she nodded. Simon's stomach hurt. She hadn't.

"You told Leila that you were being hassled and you feared for your safety so you made the men who chartered the boat all jump overboard, and towed them back to harbor."

Frankie nodded again. "That's what happened."

He had tears in his eyes again, and this time he couldn't blink them back. This time they threatened to overflow. "Dammit, tell me the truth."

She shook her head. "That *is* the truth."

"I don't believe you."

Her eyes flashed. "Okay, so I didn't go into detail. Can you really blame me for not wanting to talk about what it felt like to be *completely*, *utterly*, vulnerable? Is it my fault for not wanting to discuss what it felt like to have some awful stranger's hands in my shorts? It was easier to tell her that I was just . . . hassled."

Simon's voice felt tight. "I wouldn't call what I read in your diary *hassled*. You were sexually assaulted."

She looked down at the rug again. "Yeah," she said, her voice very quiet. "I was." She looked up at him. "But not raped."

Was she telling the truth? Simon didn't know what to believe. He looked down at the notebook she held in her hands. "You have to let me read what you wrote."

"So you'll believe me."

He nodded.

She gazed at him for a long, long time, as if deciding whether or not to let him in on her terrible secret. Finally, she handed him the notebook. "It's so nice to know I have your trust." The words were sarcastic, but her voice held only sadness. She stood up. "I need some fresh air."

Without looking back at him, Frankie walked out of the room.

Simon looked at the notebook in his hands with a feeling of dread. Slowly, he opened it. Slowly, he turned the pages to where he'd been reading.

This can't be happening. Can't be . . . He's on top of me, all two hundred and fifty pounds of him, slobbering, suffocating me, *violating* me. They're laughing as he tugs at my shorts, as the denim rips. His fingers, touching, hurting. There's nothing I can do. Powerless, numb with fear. There's nothing I can do to stop this. A fish flops near me, eyes glazing as it gasps for breath, dying, but still it struggles, still it fights to find the water.

The fish won't quit, so neither will I. My arms are pinned, but not my teeth. I bite. Fat man pulls away. One arm freed—it's all I need. One thrust up, the heel of my hand to his nose, just the way Gram taught me. Gush of blood. Howl of pain. He jerks back. I scramble free. But, God, there's five of them, and they're not laughing anymore. I make it to the flare gun, cock it, and aim it at the fat one. Everyone freezes—everyone but the last fish, still flopping on the deck. I bend down, scoop it up, and toss it overboard. Free at last. Then, standing there like some kind of wild creature, shorts torn, breasts bare and covered with the blood from the fat man's nose, I tell my merry band of fishermen to join their skinny friend in the gulf or one of 'em's gonna find out what an incandescent flare feels like, fired at close range.

And just like that it's over.

But even as I write these words, I know that from this moment on, it will never be over. From this moment on, my life will never be the same. Unlike my little fish, I'll never really be free again.

Simon slowly closed the notebook, slowly set it down on the floor.

Then he stood up and went to look for Frankie.

Simon was standing on the beach as Frankie came out of the ocean. She swept her hair back from her face, using her hands to squeeze out the water. The ocean had cooled her, cleansed her. She always felt so damn dirty if she so much as *thought* about that awful day.

The sky still held a slight hint of red-orange from the setting sun, but it was the moon, two-thirds full and waxing, that lit Simon's face.

Without his usual smile he looked older, harder, and entirely unforgiving.

"Tell me their names," he said as she stopped in

front of him, "and I'll track them down and beat the crap out of them."

Frankie moved up the beach to where the clothes she'd had on over her bathing suit were lying in a pile. "I don't remember their names."

"Like hell you don't."

She glanced back at him. With his mouth set in that grim line and his blue eyes glistening in the darkness, she could almost believe him capable of doing injury to the men who had nearly raped her all those years before. Funny, she'd never thought of Simon as the aggressive type, but he looked as if he might actually *enjoy* this particular bloody encounter.

"Why didn't you press charges?" he asked.

"There was no proof," Frankie told him, trying to sound matter-of-fact. "Preston Seaholm believed me—he told me he'd back me one hundred percent, whatever I decided to do. But the D.A. told me it's hard enough to convict someone of rape, let alone attempted rape." She heard a trace of bitterness creep into her voice. "*You* didn't take my word at face value—why should a courtroom full of strangers?"

"I'm sorry," Simon said, and he actually looked as if he were. "It's just . . . I know what you told Leila, and I had to believe that if you hadn't told her the entire truth, then you wouldn't tell me." He spoke softly, uncertainly. It was the first time Frankie had seen him with his self-assurance and supersmooth charm stripped away, with his heart laid bare.

But, no. It wasn't. The night before at the resort

restaurant she'd seen a similar look in his eyes, right after that moment when she'd been so convinced he was going to kiss her. . . .

"If you had been raped, and you hadn't even told your best friend, you damn well wouldn't have admitted it to me," Simon continued. "I mean, can you honestly stand there and tell me that you would have told me the truth?"

Frankie shook her head. He was right. She wouldn't have been able to tell him.

"That's why I had to read it myself. So don't be . . . mad at me, okay?"

Frankie nodded. Okay.

Simon nodded too. He stood there in the moonlight, just looking at her, his hands stuffed into the pockets of his shorts, his usually laughing eyes so somber and serious.

"You got any other awful secrets for me to stumble across, Francine?" he asked with only a ghost of his usual smile.

Frankie's heart was beating hard. She'd always found smooth-talking, devil-may-care Simon Hunt outrageously attractive, but knowing that he was capable of this quietness, knowing he had this vulnerability, made him damn near irresistible.

Any other awful secrets? *Only that I desperately want to feel your arms around me.* She shook her head, shivering slightly as a cool breeze blew in off the water. "No," she lied.

But it was as if he could read her mind. He stepped

toward her, taking his hands from his pockets, and drew her into his arms, wet bathing suit and all.

Frankie closed her eyes, letting her head rest on his shoulder, knowing that she'd lied to herself as well.

She wanted more from him than a comforting embrace. She wanted so much more.

SEVEN

Simon sat in his car outside Frankie's house.

This was weird.

He'd often been infatuated with women—that was nothing new. He knew how to charm his way into their lives and their beds. He was good at that. He knew how to play that game. But this time there was a twist. Yeah, he wanted into Frankie's bed. But nearly as much as he wanted that, he wanted something else. He wanted to read more of her diaries.

Yeah, it was definitely weird.

He took his cup of coffee from the cup holder and climbed out of his car.

It was seven A.M. He couldn't remember the last time he'd been up and showered and dressed this early in the morning. But Frankie had sent him home the night before, determined to sort through her diaries on her own.

Simon had been unable to sleep. He'd gotten out

of bed around 2:30 in the morning and found himself in his car, driving past Frankie's house. The lights had been on in her windows, but he didn't stop. He didn't let himself go in. He didn't dare. She'd told him in no uncertain terms that his position as her assistant was riding on his good behavior. If he came on too strong, he'd be out of the picture. And showing up on her doorstep at nearly three o'clock in the morning was definitely coming on too strong. He could make any excuse in the book, but she would know exactly why he was there.

It must have been four A.M. before he finally fell asleep. And when the phone rang a few minutes after six, he could barely mumble the word hello. But he woke up quickly enough when he realized who was on the other end of the line. It was his old friend who worked at Boston University. He'd recovered from the flu, and had come in early to catch up on missed work—and to check the computer records for Jazz Chester.

Good old Jazz had made a generous tax-deductible donation to the alumni fund just a few months earlier, before the end of the year. It was likely that the address and phone numbers Simon had scribbled on a piece of paper were current.

Simon climbed the steps to Frankie's porch. The front door was locked—the knob didn't turn in his hand, but the door wasn't latched and it swung open. He opened the screen and stepped inside.

The house was quiet, and he stopped, listening for

Frankie. Thinking she might be asleep, he moved quietly down the hall toward the kitchen.

He knew the kitchen door's hinges squeaked, so he pushed it open slowly, careful not to make too much noise as he peered inside. The light was on and the table was covered with the photocopied pages from the rental record books and several of Frankie's diaries.

Frankie's diaries.

Simon stepped into the kitchen, letting the door swing shut.

"Hey!" He jumped in alarm, sensing a flash of movement out of the corner of his eye. He turned just in time to see Frankie. She'd been standing, hidden by the door.

He met her eyes, saw the sudden shocked flash of recognition—just as the gigantic frying pan she was brandishing swung down and hit him squarely on the top of his head.

Boing. He thought it made a rather interesting sound as he dropped to his hands and knees on the kitchen floor.

"Oh, my God, *Simon!*" The frying pan clattered onto the table as Frankie knelt on the floor next to him.

He'd dropped his cup of coffee, and the steaming liquid gurgled slowly out of the small opening in the plastic lid, but Frankie only pushed it out of the way.

His ears were ringing slightly and his brain felt a touch scrambled, but she'd whacked him where his skull was particularly thick. He'd hit his head far harder before with only a small lump to show for it. He would probably be tender for a few days, but it wasn't really that big a deal.

But Frankie didn't know that. She cupped his face with cool fingers, her eyes dark with concern. "Oh, Si, are you all right?"

Her face was inches away from his as she helped him down so that he was lying on his back. She leaned even closer to run her fingers lightly across his head, searching for the spot where she'd hit him.

Despite the bump on his head, it felt sinfully good. He could smell her sweet scent—some kind of herbal shampoo, the warm aroma of coffee on her breath, a hint of sunscreen and her own unmistakable and very female perfume. She was kneeling next to him, her thigh pressed against his hip, fingers in his hair. It was entirely possible that he'd died and gone to heaven.

"I better get you some ice," Frankie said.

He didn't need any ice. Not for his head anyway. It was other parts of his anatomy that could use cooling down. But she was back beside him in a flash, lifting his head onto her lap.

He was okay. The ringing in his ears was almost entirely gone and his knees no longer felt rubbery. But the ice pack felt good against his slightly bruised scalp, as did her fingers in his hair. Her other hand gently stroked the side of his face, and his cheek pressed against the softness of her belly. . . . Oh, this was too good an opportunity to pass up.

Simon let his eyelids flutter shut.

"Oh, no," Frankie said, worry in her voice.

"You're not supposed to go to sleep with a head injury. Come on, you better sit up while I call Doc Devlin."

Simon let his muscles go limp.

"Simon?" She tried pushing him up, but without his cooperation he was too difficult to move. He felt her lower his head to the floor, and then move around in front of him. She tugged at his shoulders, trying to pull him into a sitting position. "Come on, Si, talk to me. How did you get in here? Dammit, you scared me to death. The door was locked. I always lock up at night."

"Wasn't latched," Simon murmured. "Sorry I scared you, honey. . . ."

Honey. The last time he'd called her that, she'd damn near had a heart attack. She'd given him a two-hour-long speech on sexist terms of endearment. This time she didn't say a word.

She tugged harder at his shoulders, finally straddling his legs to get more leverage. She gripped him tightly, all of her muscles straining.

"What are you doing up this early anyway?" she asked.

Simon let her pull him up, but then wobbled slightly so that she'd have to hold him tightly. She did, her breasts pressed against his chest, her arms around his back, her thighs gripping his hips. It felt too intensely good. He couldn't keep a strangled sound of pleasure from escaping.

"Does it hurt that bad?"

Hurt? Not exactly . . .

"Simon, come on. Open your eyes and talk to me!"

Simon opened his eyes and knew he'd gone too far. Her expression was filled with anxiety and concern, and her eyes were brimming with worried tears.

"Hey." He reached up to blot a tear that had caught on her eyelash. "Hey, I'm really okay, Francine. The ice is working, and you didn't hit me *that* hard."

She pulled back slightly, lifting his chin to look more closely into his eyes. What she saw made her own eyes narrow. "You were faking," she breathed. "You son of a bitch! I can't believe it. I thought I nearly killed you, and you were *faking* it."

Simon gave her his best smile. "At least I'm not going to die, right?"

"Don't count on it," Frankie muttered.

"Next time use a cast iron frying pan," he advised her. "Aluminum just doesn't cut it."

"Shoot, Simon, that was just plain mean. Why would you make me think that . . ."

Her voice trailed off and her eyes widened a little as she realized the intimacy of their position. She sat, frozen, gazing at him, awareness in her eyes.

The sudden heat was incredible. It crackled around them, a furnace blast of sexual fire unlike anything Simon had felt in close to an eternity. Time slowed and stretched out, each second seeming like a lifetime as she gazed into his eyes.

Holding her this way felt so good, so right. She was a perfect fit in his arms, and he knew she felt it too. But slowly, almost jerkily, she pushed herself off him, and the moment was gone.

She'd been up all night. She was still wearing the same shorts and T-shirt she'd had on the evening before. She was still wearing her bathing suit underneath her clothes. She stood up and poured a cup of coffee from the pot on the counter, bringing the mug of steaming liquid to her mouth with a shaking hand.

"What *are* you doing here so early?" she asked.

Jazz Chester's address and phone numbers seemed to burn in Simon's pocket. If he as much as mentioned Jazz's name . . . What was he thinking? That if he mentioned Jazz's name he might as well kiss good-bye his chance of making it with Francine? The truth was, he had no chance to start with, at least not just then. Hell, she'd pulled an all-nighter reading her diary entries from Jazz Chester's early visits to Sunrise Key. Simon would have no chance with Francine until she found Jazz and found out that real life rarely holds up to fantasies.

She wasn't unaffected by this encounter, Simon knew that. But he also knew without a doubt that pushing the issue would be a major mistake.

But Frankie didn't give him time to answer. "I was just about to crawl into bed—defeated." She picked up his travel mug from the floor and used a sponge to mop up the spilled coffee. "I narrowed the list of men named John down to three," she explained. "John Marshall, John McMahon, and John Carter. But when I double-checked the phone numbers with directory assistance, none of them was right. All three of these men moved years ago—and there's no way to get their forwarding addresses or phone numbers." She sighed. "Did you know there are forty-seven John Carters in Baltimore? And another seventeen J. Carters too. That's assuming our John Carter even lives in Baltimore anymore. Heck, he could be *any*where."

Simon pulled himself to his feet, setting the ice pack down near the sink as he took Jazz's phone number and address from his pocket and handed it to Frankie.

She stared at it: "217 Oxen Yoke Road, Wellesley— What's this?"

"Tim finally called."

She looked at him blankly. "Tim?"

"My friend who works at Boston University." Simon refilled his mug with coffee and took a sip.

Frankie stared at the piece of paper. "Is this . . . ?"

"Jazz Chester's address and phone numbers—both home and work. It's current—at least as of four months ago."

"I don't know whether to kill you or kiss you."

Simon laughed, raking his hair back from his face, wincing as his fingers touched the lump on his head. "I don't seem to have any problem with that decision, if you want me to make it for you."

"No, thanks." She quickly looked away from him, as if suddenly remembering the sensation of his body against hers. God knows, Simon was remembering it. It was damned difficult to think about anything else.

She looked down at the paper again, looking at it

as if it were both a winning lottery ticket and a warrant for her arrest. "Suddenly I'm scared to death."

"Do you want me to call him?"

"No, I can do this. I *want* to do this." She squared her shoulders and risked another look in his direction. "In fact, if you'll give me some privacy, I'm going to call him right now."

Simon glanced at his watch. "It's not even eight o'clock. Are you sure—"

"Jazz was a morning person. I'm betting he still is, and that he's already at his office," Frankie said. She picked up the kitchen phone and gave Simon a pointed look. "If you don't mind . . . ?"

Simon didn't want to leave. He wanted to stay. And listen. "I guess I'll be in your office."

"With your ear pressed to the wall? I don't think so," Frankie said. "Why don't you head home? I'll call you later."

Simon crossed his arms. "No way am I leaving without stepfather John's phone number. Remember me? I've got a client to keep happy too."

"There's no way *you're* getting John's phone number before Clay Quinn does," Frankie countered.

She was right. It would be unprofessional and unacceptable. And it had nothing to do with the real reason he wanted to stay.

"I'm sorry, you're right," he admitted. "It's just . . ." He trailed off, out of excuses.

"I know I'm not the only one who stands to make a lot of money on this deal," she said, "but I'm not thinking about the money right now."

He wasn't either, but he wasn't sure she'd believe him if he told her the truth.

"This boy used to mean the world to me," Frankie continued, waving the piece of paper with Jazz's phone numbers. "If you want to know the truth, I believe I was truly in love with him. Leila once told me that she thought I was secretly still in love with Jazz, still waiting for him to come back, even after all these years. For all I know, she could very well be right." She took a deep breath. "But what I *do* know is that I don't need you and your games to get in my way."

His *games*. Her words stung particularly harshly, because he knew they were true. He *did* play games. His entire life was one giant game—never too serious and not particularly hard to win since he alone was responsible for writing and rewriting the rules. He was silent. What could he possibly say?

"Can you try to understand, just a little bit?"

"Yeah." He understood. More than she'd believe. He took his mug of coffee from the counter and pushed open the kitchen door. "I'll be on the beach." He paused, looking back at her, wishing his stomach weren't in a knot, praying that Jazz Chester was married, or a priest, or gay, and at the same time praying that the man was everything Frankie wanted him to be, everything she needed. She deserved happiness, and he knew that he himself—he and his *games*—couldn't bring her that. He tried to smile, hoping the words he was about to say weren't going to stick in his throat. "Good luck."

She'd never know how much it had cost him to say that. She'd never know that his heart felt as if it were breaking in two.

The door closed gently behind him as she began to dial the phone.

Frankie closed her eyes, listening to the telephone ring. It rang four times and then clicked over to an answering machine.

She didn't know whether to feel relieved or alarmed. She was going to have to leave a message. What was she going to say?

"Hi, this is Jonathan Chester. I'm away from my desk right now. Leave a message and I'll get back to you as soon as I can."

It was Jazz. He called himself Jonathan—Frankie hadn't realized that was his real name—but the voice on the tape was Jazz's. His voice sounded deeper, richer, older, and more restrained, but it was still musical and pleasant, as if he were smiling while he spoke.

The phone beeped. It was Frankie's turn to talk.

"Hi, um, Jazz? My name is Francine Paresky, and I'm calling from Sunrise Key, down in Florida. I don't know if you remember me, but—"

There was a click and the phone was picked up. "Frankie?" It was Jazz. "My God, is that *you*?"

Frankie laughed, suddenly giddy with relief. "Yeah," she said. "It's me."

"I'm sorry I didn't pick up right away," Jazz told her in a voice that sounded a whole lot less grown-up than the voice on the tape, "but when I come in to work this early in the morning, I screen my calls, and . . . *God*, how are you?"

"I'm . . . I'm okay. I'm good." After all these years, she was talking to *Jazz* again. She felt both hot and cold and decidedly weak in the knees. She sat down at the kitchen table, playing with the curled telephone wire, stretching it out and then releasing it, watching it bounce. "Older. I'm older." A movement out the window caught her eye. Simon. Walking on the beach.

Jazz's laugh was rich and warm. "Yeah, me too. You know—this is really crazy. You're going to think I'm nuts, but I was just thinking about you. Not more than two days ago. Isn't that *wild*?"

He sounded exactly the same. He still spoke with that same underlying sense of urgency and excitement, as if the words he spoke and the person he spoke to were the most important in all the world. It *was* wild. It was as if she'd suddenly been thrust into a time warp and sent back a dozen years into the past.

Frankie tried to picture Jazz, but oddly enough her mind kept turning his clean, all-American features into Simon's more angular, almost elegant face, his brown hair into blond. She turned away from the window, suddenly aware that she was still gazing at Simon—a romantic solitary figure looking out over the waves.

"I was watching a movie," Jazz continued, "and this girl, I swear, she's gorgeous—she looks *exactly* like you. Marisa something. She's in everything these days.

Honest, Frankie, the first time I saw her, I was sure it *was* you."

Frankie smiled, rolling her eyes. "Thanks for the compliment, Jazz, but I think maybe you don't remember me all that clearly."

"Oh, yes, I do. I have extremely vivid memories of you." He spoke softly, pausing just long enough to make her recall her *own* vivid memories. Long, slow kisses on the beach . . . But just like that, his voice changed and he was upbeat and friendly again. "So come on. Tell me what you're up to these days. Probably married with a pack of adorable kids, right? Come on, 'fess up, babe. Break my heart."

Frankie's gaze slid back to the window. Simon hadn't moved. The wind tousled his blond hair. *Break my heart.* When Simon had left her so she could make this phone call, he'd looked at her with the oddest expression on his face. It was almost as if she were breaking *his* heart. But she knew that couldn't be true. Simon's heart was made of Tyvek. It was indestructible.

"Frankie, you still there?"

Lord, what was she doing? Letting her mind wander to Simon while she was on the phone with Jazz . . . "No, I'm not married—"

"No? That's hard to believe."

"How about you?"

"Me? I'm . . . still as footloose as ever. I tried marriage for a while, but things, you know, change. But that's not fair. We were talking about *you*. Come on, fill me in on the past ten years. Don't leave out any details."

"You're working—I don't want to take up too much of your time—"

"Are you kidding? I've got my priorities straight—and old friends win out over early morning busywork any day."

Jazz wasn't married. He wasn't married, and he was still the nicest guy in the world. She looked out the window again, but Simon had disappeared.

"I still live on Sunrise Key," Frankie said. She told him the entire story. Clay Quinn's visit. Alice Winfield's death. The will. Her search for his stepfather. Jazz listened intently, interrupting occasionally with a sympathetic comment or a lighthearted joke that made her laugh.

But the entire time she spoke, she watched out the window, wondering where Simon had gone, and waiting for him to return.

EIGHT

"What are you doing? Where did you get that?"

Simon was on the beach, sitting on the sand out of sight of the house, reading one of Frankie's diaries. He jumped about a mile into the air at the sound of her voice, then tried to hide the notebook he'd been reading so intently.

"I don't believe you." Frankie held out her hand for the notebook. "Leila always claimed you were the nosiest brother in the world, but I didn't believe her—until now."

He managed to look abashed, but on Simon the effect was disgustingly charming. "I'm sorry." He handed it to her and pulled her down next to him on the sand at the same time. "I couldn't resist. It was on the floor in the hall, and I . . ." He shrugged. "I'm addicted."

"To my diaries," Frankie said flatly.

"It's awful. I can't seem to get enough."

Frankie flipped open the cover. "I wrote this when I was *twelve*. Was it really that fascinating?"

Simon laughed. "Yeah. You were a scream. Some of the things you said . . ."

"Oh, Lord, should I dig a hole and bury myself in it now?"

His eyes were the same color as the sunlit ocean, and when he laughed again, they sparkled even brighter. "No way. It's great stuff, Francine. Like . . . you had this plan to end the cold war. It was great. Each family in the United States had to exchange one child with a family in Russia. You figured no one on either side would dare start a nuclear war when one of their kids was behind enemy lines."

Frankie had to smile. "I remember that. I bet it would've worked too."

"That was almost as good as your plan for racial harmony," Simon told her with a grin. "You figured if everyone who was white was required to marry someone nonwhite and vice versa, within a generation or two we'd all be the same color."

"That works well in theory," Frankie admitted, "but at age twelve I didn't know too much about the workings of love and freedom of choice. *Requiring* people to marry . . . it's unconstitutional."

"In some ways, life was much simpler at age twelve," Simon said. "In other ways, it was incredibly complex. Two weeks after you wrote that particular forward-thinking diatribe on social reform, you proclaimed exactly who you and Leila were going to marry."

Frankie closed her eyes, scrunching her nose in an expression of dread. "I'm afraid to ask."

"You don't remember? I'm crushed." Simon leaned back in the sand, supporting himself on his elbows. The ocean breeze blew a lock of hair in his face and then pushed it away. "You decided that Leila would marry Marsh Devlin."

He smiled at the expression of surprise Frankie knew was on her face. "Wow. Just call me Nostradamus," she said. "How could I possibly have predicted *that*? Leila despised Marsh back then. What was I thinking?"

"You weren't thinking. From what you wrote, I'm guessing it was some kind of early hormonal reaction."

"To what?" Frankie glanced down at Simon, surprised to see embarrassment in his eyes. He looked away first, squinting as he stared out at the ocean.

"You honestly don't remember?"

She shook her head.

"Well . . . to me, actually. Since Marsh was my best friend, you figured it would work out rather neatly if Leila married him. Because you decided that you were going to marry *me*."

When their eyes met, something caught and sparked. Frankie felt hypnotized. She stared at him, unable to look away, unable to move, unable to think about anything but the way she had held him so tightly, her body pressed intimately against his, just a short time ago. Lord, she still had some kind of raging hormonal reaction to the man. Some things never changed.

As she watched, Simon wet his lips as if they were suddenly too dry. It was a nervous movement. Simon, nervous?

"You saw me shooting hoops down by the town beach." His voice was raspy and he stopped to clear his throat. "Apparently my incredible teenage splendor made your twelve-year-old hormones kick in." He was trying to joke, but his words didn't counteract the hunger Frankie saw in his eyes. He must have realized that, too, because he made himself look away. "You wrote in your diary that you were riding your bike, and it was the weirdest thing. You looked over and saw me, Leila's big brother, Simon, playing basketball. No big deal. But then you looked again, and suddenly it wasn't just Simon, it was *Simon*. I know exactly what it felt like, because the same thing happened to me the summer you turned eighteen."

"Oh, yeah, right."

Simon met her eyes again, and she could not for the life of her figure out if he was teasing or serious.

"You and Leila were walking toward me on the beach," he told her. "I saw you coming, and I started thinking, Leila and Frankie want a ride someplace. I started trying to think up excuses and reasons why I couldn't drive you where you wanted to go. But in the time it took you to walk up to me and past me, I'm looking at you and *looking* at you and I'm thinking that's Frankie. That's Frankie? Oh, man, that's *Frankie*."

Frankie laughed, shaking her head, unable to react any other way. She couldn't believe what he was saying. How *could* she?

"Of course, I have no proof," Simon continued. "I didn't keep a diary."

"How convenient for you." Frankie stood up and brushed the sand from her bottom. "If fairy-tale hour is over, I've got to go get packed."

"Fairy tale?" Simon said. "Oh, man, I share my deepest secrets with you and you have the audacity to call them *fairy* tales?"

He actually managed to look hurt. Frankie had to remind herself that this was Simon Hunt she was dealing with. Somehow he'd gotten it stuck in his mind that she was going to be his next sexual conquest. She had to remember that he'd say or do damn near anything to achieve his goal.

But she knew how to make him back away, and back away fast.

She lifted her chin as she looked down at him, still sitting there in the sand. "You want to make my predictions two for two?" she asked. "We could do a double wedding with Leila and Marsh."

But he knew she was only bluffing, and he smiled and called her on it. "Why wait? We could fly to Vegas tonight."

"Sorry, I can't," Frankie said coolly, annoyed that she hadn't managed to make him squirm. "In about three hours I'm catching a flight up to Boston."

Simon sat up straight. "Boston?"

"I'm having dinner with Jazz tonight."

The look of incredulousness on Simon's face nearly duplicated her own emotional state. It seemed crazy, unlikely, impossible. But it was true. After too many years apart, she was going to see Jazz Chester. Tonight. So what was she doing, standing there playing games with Simon Hunt? She should just walk away. She should turn around and go to Boston and never come back—at least not without Jazz.

"Whoa." Simon looked out at the horizon as if he needed its steadying influence. "I guess you got through to him."

Frankie nodded. "He was in his office."

Simon stood up, brushing the sand from the seat of his shorts. "And you're going there *today*?"

"I'm catching the ten-fifty flight off the island."

"Tell me about the phone call. Start with the part where he said hello."

"He's exactly the same," Frankie told him. "He's single—divorced, I think. He didn't go into detail. I told him about my search for his stepfather—Marshall is John's last name. We were close, tracking him with the rental records."

"So that's it? Case closed? Time for a vacation in Boston?"

"The case isn't closed." Frankie started walking back toward the house, and he followed. "Jazz didn't have John Marshall's phone number—they didn't stay in touch. Jazz's mother and John were divorced twelve years ago. That's why Jazz never came back to Sunrise Key."

Simon snorted. "Is that what he told you? And you believed him?"

Frankie shot him a hard look. "Of course."

"He was what, twenty years old, yet he couldn't come down here without his mommy and his daddy?"

"Sunrise Key was John's favorite vacation spot," Frankie said tightly. "Jazz *wanted* to come back, but he was afraid he'd run into John. Apparently the divorce was nasty."

Simon lifted one eyebrow. "It looks bad to me, Francine. He can't be *bothered* to come back here, yet at the drop of a hat you're blowing hundreds of bucks on a plane ticket to see *him* again. He's taking advantage of you."

Frankie stopped on the stairs to the back porch feeling exasperated and annoyed and emotionally chafed. What did she care what Simon thought? And certainly, who was he to criticize Jazz? Simon hadn't had a single relationship in his entire life that wasn't based on his taking advantage of someone else's hopes and emotions and weaknesses. He hadn't *once* had a relationship where he'd been the one to give instead of take, where *he'd* been the one to fly a thousand miles, his heart in his throat, simply to see someone's smile.

"For your information," she said icily, "my trip to Boston isn't a social call. Jazz's mother *did* keep in touch with John Marshall regarding alimony payments. Jazz thinks Marshall's current phone number is in her address book."

"And you can't just call her . . . ?"

"No, I can't. She died six months ago."

He was instantly contrite. "I'm sorry, I didn't know—"

"There's a lot you don't know."

"You're right. I'm sorry. Please, fill me in."

"Jazz hasn't had time to go through his mother's personal effects," Frankie said stiffly. "Everything from her apartment was packed up and put in one of those self-storage facilities. He thinks there's at least one, maybe two boxes that are labeled as being from her desk."

Simon looked at his watch. "Okay. What do I need to pack? How many days do you think we'll have to stay?"

"We?"

"I'm coming too."

Frankie had to laugh. "Oh, no, you're not. I don't need your help for this."

"What if John Marshall's address *isn't* in the box that was packed from Jazz's mom's desk? What if you need to search through the entire storage area? You'll need me for that."

"I'll muddle through."

"I'll meet you at the airport at ten-thirty." Simon started walking toward the front of the house, toward the street where his car was parked. "Until this case is closed, I'm your assistant, remember?"

"No, you're not my assistant." Frankie chased after him. She had to go to Boston alone. It would be too weird to see Jazz for the first time in years with Simon looking on.

"Oh, yes, I am."

Frankie's frustration turned to full-blown annoyance. "Look, Si, this was just another one of your games, but it's over now. You lose—I didn't sleep with you. Sorry. Time to hit on your next target."

Simon looked at her over the top of his sports car, a deadly glint in his eye. If Frankie hadn't known better, she might have thought he was even more upset about this than she was. "Are you kidding?" he said with a tight smile. "This isn't over—it's just starting to get interesting. See you at the airport, boss." He got into his car, closing the door behind him and starting the engine with a roar.

Frankie's annoyance turned to anger, and she leaned down, knocking rapidly on the passenger's side window until he opened it. "You're fired. You can't come with me because you're *fired*!"

He just laughed as he slipped his sunglasses onto his nose and drove away.

Simon had to pull over to the side of Ocean Avenue. He had to take several long, slow, deep breaths before his heart rate returned to near normal and his hands stopped shaking.

Jazz was single. Jazz was exactly as Frankie had remembered him. Jazz was friggin' *perfect*.

Jazz was going to have dinner with her tonight. . . .

It was his worst nightmare coming true. God help him, if Jazz truly turned out to be a candidate for

Mister Rogers's nice-guy-of-the-year award, Simon could quite literally kiss Frankie good-bye.

He could see it all so clearly. She'd extend her trip to Boston for a week or two. Before the second week was out, Jazz, not being stupid enough to pass up a good thing twice, would ask her to marry him. And Simon would be a guest at their June wedding. He'd sit in the back of the church and die a thousand times, wanting her, *needing* her, knowing she was forever out of his reach.

Of course, he'd finally get his chance to kiss Frankie—when he kissed Jazz's bride.

Just like that, Frankie would be gone forever.

You're fired, she'd told him.

Like hell he was.

You lose.

Not yet, he didn't. Not yet, not by a long shot.

He *was* going to Boston. And before midnight tonight, he vowed, he was going to seduce her. He was going to get what he wanted and convince Frankie that it was what *she* wanted too. All it would take was a single kiss.

He was a fool for not having kissed her before. He'd had the opportunity. One kiss and she'd stop being able to hide the fact that she wanted him as badly as he wanted her. One kiss and this mutual attraction they'd both denied for so long would ignite into flames.

One kiss . . .

Nothing and no one was going to stop him.

No one except Jazz Chester. Nothing except the

fact that Jazz was the one Frankie truly wanted. Jazz was the one who was going to be with her tonight, holding her, kissing her, probably even making love to her.

Miserably, Simon pulled his car back onto Ocean Avenue and drove the rest of the way home.

NINE

The phone rang in the hotel room, and Frankie dove across the king-sized bed to pick it up. "Hello?"

It wasn't Simon.

It was the starchy-sounding concierge from the hotel's front desk. "Several large boxes have been delivered for you," he said, his blue-blooded voice tinged with disapproval. "Shall I have the bellboy bring them up?"

"Yes, thank you."

She hung up the phone, silently berating herself. Of course it wouldn't be Simon on the phone. Simon hadn't bothered to show up for the airline flight off the key. Apparently, he'd thought better of their parting argument, and cut his losses. No doubt he'd moved on—exactly as she'd said—to his next "target."

No, he wouldn't be calling her here. Besides, even if he *did* do something as certifiably insane as follow her to Boston on a later flight, there was no way he'd find her at the ritzy Parker House hotel.

Frankie had called Clayton Quinn on her flight from Orlando to Boston. She'd filled her client in, letting him know she was close to finding his great-aunt Alice's mysterious friend John. Clay had been thrilled at her progress. He'd been ecstatic at the news she'd discovered John's last name was Marshall, and that his current phone number and address were—hopefully—packed in a box in Boston.

Clay had recommended that Frankie stay at the Parker House while she was in Boston. In fact, he had more than recommended—he'd insisted. He'd reminded her to keep her receipts for lodging and meals. Whatever she spent would be reimbursed as a travel expense.

She'd made her room reservation from the plane, and had been shocked to find out that one night's stay in the fancy hotel cost more than she normally spent on four weeks' worth of groceries.

The towels were heated on steam-filled bars in the bathroom. There were telephones in every corner of the room. Huge windows overlooked downtown Boston. The furniture and decor were elegant and made Frankie feel a touch nervous—as if she might accidentally break something priceless.

No, Simon would never think to look for her here.

There was a knock on the door—the bellboy with the boxes sent over from the storage facility. He frowned, recognizing her from the front desk, where she'd insisted on carrying her own small suitcase up to her room. Still, he was servitude incarnate, making sure he placed the boxes exactly, precisely where she wanted them, and offering to open them for her. Frankie tipped him—too little from the look on his face—and then he was gone.

She closed the door and turned to gaze at the big boxes. Somewhere inside one of those boxes were a phone number and an address that were going to solve her first big-league case *and* get her that $10,000 bonus.

So why didn't she feel excited? Why wasn't she giddy with euphoria? Why wasn't she doing a victory dance and slapping a high five?

Well, there wasn't anyone to high-five, for starters. Simon should have been with her.

Frankie shook her head. Where had *that* crazy thought come from? She certainly didn't need Simon around, distracting her with his bedroom eyes. No, she didn't need Simon, subtly stealing her focus away from everyone and everything else around her, until all she thought about was his smile, the sound of his laughter, the touch of his hand on her arm, the look in his eyes as he undressed her. . . .

And *that* was one fantasy she was never going to live out. Simon had given up on her. True, she'd fired him, but when had something like that ever stopped him before? It was clear he'd decided she simply wasn't worth the effort.

Dear Lord, she was exhausted. She'd been up all night. She'd caught a few hours of sleep on the plane, but she wasn't a happy flyer, and her nerves kept her from feeling truly rested.

No, this wasn't disappointment she was feeling, it was fatigue. Simon Hunt was nothing but trouble, and she was a thousand miles away from that trouble right now, and that was a *good* thing. Wasn't it?

Jazz. Think about Jazz, not Simon.

She had approximately thirty minutes to shower and transform herself into something that looked more alive than dead before Jazz Chester came to take her to dinner.

Frankie pulled out the blue-flowered dress she'd thrown into her suitcase along with a clean pair of jeans, a few extra T-shirts, and several changes of underwear.

When she'd called Jazz from the hotel, he told her he'd have his secretary make a reservation for dinner at the restaurant right there in the Parker House. Frankie had caught a glimpse of the restaurant from the front desk. It was *not* a jeans-and-T-shirt kind of place.

Only someone with Simon's confidence and charisma could walk into a fancy restaurant wearing blue jeans and a T-shirt and look as if he were properly dressed. Simon had that slightly amused, so-what attitude. . . .

Frankie skimmed off her clothes and climbed into the shower. She closed her eyes and let the water pound down on her head.

So what. It was a good attitude to have, and in her current state, not impossible to adopt.

So what if she was having dinner with the first boy she'd ever loved. So what if she didn't feel like wearing some stupid wrinkled dress. So what if the restaurant didn't serve her because she was wearing jeans and a T-shirt—they'd go get pizza. So what if Jazz disapproved . . .

And if she never even so much as *saw* Simon again . . .

Try as hard as she might, when it came to Simon Hunt, Frankie couldn't summon up a single so-what.

"I'm sorry," the hotel concierge told Simon. "I can't give out room numbers for our guests, but I can connect you to Ms. Paresky's room."

Simon had a pinpoint spot of pain directly over his left eyebrow that was threatening to explode into the biggest headache he'd ever had in his life. It had started before he'd sat in traffic for more than forty-five minutes in the taxi that took him from Logan Airport to the Parker House. It had started before the flight he took from Sarasota was delayed for two hours. It had started before he'd been unable to charter a plane off Sunrise Key and had had to rent a car and drive all the way to the Sarasota airport. It had started when he'd realized he was going to miss the 10:50 flight off the key, when he'd stopped to play the messages on his answering machine. One of his best clients had left half a dozen distressed calls about several priceless twelfth-century pieces she was trying to unload to a buyer in Jacksonville who hadn't done more than give her a verbal commitment.

He'd returned the call, calming the elderly lady down and promising to get the agreement in writing as soon as he returned from Boston. But his client was so upset—her grandson's college education depended on this sale—he had to draw up a written agreement. It had to be faxed to both the seller and the buyer and reworded and refaxed, and before Simon stood up from his desk, it was just after eleven. The sale was binding, his client was relieved, but he'd missed Frankie's flight.

And here he was. In Boston. Frankie had had a ten-minute jump on him leaving the key, but she'd gotten to the hotel a solid five hours earlier. It was nearly seven-thirty now. Please God, Simon prayed as he picked up the extension the concierge offered him and listened to the phone ring up in Frankie's room, please let Jazz be fashionably late for their dinner date.

But the phone rang and rang and rang.

"I'm sorry, sir," the man said without a whit of apology in his expression, "the young lady is not in her room at this time."

It was entirely possible that Simon was too late.

Frankie was with Jazz right now.

Oh, God, he was too late.

Simon knew exactly what he'd do if he took Frankie out to dinner. He'd bring her someplace nice, somewhere with music—a band or piano player. In between the salad course and the soup, he'd pull her out onto the dance floor and take her into his arms.

She'd fit against him perfectly as they danced, and he'd close his eyes, reveling in the full body contact. But before the song ended, he'd lean down and claim her lips in a slow, lingering, delicious kiss. He'd dance with her again and again, and before dessert and coffee arrived, he'd stand up, but this time they wouldn't go onto the dance floor. This time they'd leave the restaurant, go to his hotel room . . .

Jazz was no fool. If Frankie was even the least bit willing, Simon wasn't going to see her until late the next morning, after she spent the night with Jazz.

Man, he felt sick.

The concierge was eyeing him nervously. No doubt he hadn't missed the sudden tears that had sprung into Simon's eyes.

"I'm really disappointed," Simon admitted to the man. "See, I've got it bad for this lady, but I got here too late and now she's out with some real butt-head. I'm afraid she's going to fall in love with this guy, and that's making it hard for me to breathe, you know? I didn't expect to feel this way, and I'm scared to death."

To his surprise, the concierge nodded, compassion in his normally expressionless eyes. And when he spoke, his upper-crust accent was gone. "Can I getcha anything, pal?" the man asked in a thick local Boston accent.

"A room and stiff drink or six," Simon said miserably. "Not necessarily in that order."

"If you trust me with your driver's license and a credit card," the man said, "you can head on into the bar and I'll bring 'em back to you with a room key in less than five minutes. You can leave your luggage behind the counter too. I'll have it sent up to your room."

Simon took both cards from his wallet and placed them on the counter. He leaned forward to read the man's name tag. "Thanks, Dominic."

He turned toward the bar, but the concierge stopped him. "Hey, Mr. Hunt." Simon turned back. "At the risk of not minding my own business, I gotta tell you, pal, you might stand a better chance of finding the lady *without* the drinks."

It was a good point. "Do you live here in Boston?" Simon asked the man.

He nodded. "Have for all my life."

"Where would *you* take a woman out to dinner if you really wanted to impress her?"

The concierge smiled. "Attaboy. I knew you weren't a quitter. I'll make you a list and call you a guy I know, drives a cab. Meanwhile, why don't you start with the obvious? We got a four-star restaurant right here in the hotel."

"I really appreciate it, Dominic."

Dominic nodded. "There used to be a girl I loved the way you love yours, but I let her get away. Not a day goes by that I don't regret that."

He turned to his computer screen, leaving Simon staring at him.

Love . . . ? Who said anything about . . . *love*?

Sure, he was upset at the thought of losing Frankie to Jazz. . . . But *love*?

No, it couldn't be. Could it?

Simon stopped just inside the entrance to the hotel's crowded restaurant, letting his eyes get accustomed to the romantic lighting. Music was playing. A trio was set up in the corner of the room, and they were performing an old standard. It was slow, romantic, and easy to dance to. The dance floor was near the band, and a number of couples swayed in time to the music.

Simon searched the faces for Frankie. She wasn't on the dance floor. And she wasn't sitting at the tables nearby. She wasn't near a small bar that occupied another corner of the room She wasn't . . .

She was.

She was *there*. She was sitting at one of the secluded tables near the windows. She was wearing some kind of a white shirt and her hair was brushed back from her face and—

She laughed at something Jazz Chester said, and Simon felt his heart lodge in his throat. Dear God, she looked so beautiful. When she smiled, the entire world seemed to light up around her.

He loved her. Dominic was right. It *was* love. Simon was totally, mind-blowingly, completely in love with Francine Paresky. He had to sit down. . . .

"May I help you, sir?" The maître d' stepped in front of him as he headed toward one of the empty seats at the bar.

"I need a drink."

"I'm sorry, sir," the man said loftily, "but after

seven-thirty our bar is closed to all but dinner service. There's another bar across the lobby—"

"No," Simon said. On the other side of the room, Jazz Chester, damn his eyes, reached across the small table and took Frankie's hand. On this side of the room Simon could do little more than watch. Jazz didn't know her, not the way Simon did. Jazz had never read Frankie's diaries. Jazz didn't even know that she wrote down her every thought, every wish, every desire. But Simon did.

Simon knew from the way Jazz was looking at Frankie that the man's number-one priority was to get inside her pants, not her head. Sure, Simon had his own sexual agenda, but there was so much more to what he was feeling than that. He wanted to be with her, to talk to her, to watch her eyes as she talked to him, as she told him her secrets.

Oh, God. He loved Frankie. How had this happened? When had this become more than a game?

"Perhaps you'd like a table . . . ?" the maître d' asked.

Simon pulled his gaze away from Frankie and forced himself to smile. This guy was a real load. "Preferably one with a seat, please."

"There's a forty-minute wait for a table," the maître d' told him with barely concealed sadistic pleasure. "Perhaps you'd enjoy a walk around the block, or a seat in the hotel lobby?"

Simon shook his head. "No, you don't understand—"

At that moment the concierge appeared at Simon's elbow.

"Any luck, sir?" he asked, his fake upper-crust accent securely back in place.

Simon nodded. "She's here, Dom, but there's a forty-minute wait for a table."

The concierge looked at the maître d'. "Mr. Hunt can be seated at the bar, Robert."

"I'm sorry, Mr. Defeo." The maître d's lips were tightly pressed together. "But as I told this gentleman, the bar is closed."

Dominic lifted an eyebrow. "Then . . . open it."

"But it's after seven-thirty and we've got only one bartender on duty." He sniffed primly. "The rules *clearly* state no paying customers at the bar after—"

Dominic leaned closer, lowering his voice, dropping his accent. "Seat him at the bar, you rigid idiot, and give him his drink on the house—that way he's not a paying customer and everyone's happy."

The maître d's mouth opened in a silent oh. "Seat him yourself," he said, walking away in a huff.

Dom tapped his forehead. "Creative thinking, Bobby," he called after him. "You should try it sometime." He handed Simon his credit card, driver's license, and a room key as he led him to the bar. "Good luck," he said. "Let me know how it all turns out."

Simon clasped the older man's hand. "Thanks. I will."

"Hey, Vinnie," Dominic said to the bartender. "Set my friend here up—but keep his drinks watered down. He's gonna need his wits about him."

"Sure thing, Mr. Defeo."

"Just a ginger ale, Vinnie." Simon was looking at Frankie, and Dominic followed his gaze.

"That her?" he asked.

Simon nodded. "Yeah."

As the two men watched, Jazz Chester stood up. He tugged at Frankie's hand and she rose gracefully from the table. Together they moved onto the dance floor.

Simon heard Dominic chuckle. "How'd she manage to get past Mr. Rules and Regulations wearing jeans?"

The bartender put a glass of ginger ale down on the bar near Simon's elbow. "Bob told me she told *him* she was some kind of famous movie star," he said. "That's why he waived the dress code. I'm also supposed to keep an eye out for paparazzi. Run interference if necessary."

Dominic looked at Simon questioningly, his bushy eyebrows raised. "A famous movie star?"

Simon laughed, shaking his head no. "She's like you—a creative thinker. She's a private investigator who lives on the west coast of Florida. She moonlights as a cabdriver."

"She looks kind of like what's-her-name," Vinnie said. "You know the girl I mean. Good actress."

"The one who's in all the pictures these days," Dom said. "Italian-sounding name. Very pretty girl."

Simon fell silent, watching Frankie and Jazz dance. Frankie was actually wearing jeans and a plain white T-shirt. She had cowboy boots on her feet. Cowboy boots and faded jeans in a four-star restaurant . . . Her jeans fit her snugly, hugging her compact, slender body in a way that had turned his head for years. For years he'd been content to watch her walk away from him, but that was going to stop right there and right then.

Jazz pulled her closer, and she shut her eyes, resting her head on his shoulder.

Simon's heart sank. She looked so peaceful, so content. Jazz Chester was as handsome as Simon had remembered him. His brown hair was darker and he'd filled out, but he was still in good shape. His picture-perfect features had thickened a bit, but the effect only made him better-looking, more rugged.

According to Frankie, Jazz was the nicest guy in the world. Simon had never been accused of that in his entire life.

"She looks happy," Simon whispered.

"Wait a minute. What's with this noble-sacrifice crap?" Dominic asked in disbelief. "You're not gonna pull some kind of I-love-her-enough-to-let-her-go stupid-ass stunt here, are you?"

As Simon watched, Jazz pulled Frankie's lips up to his own and kissed her slowly, tenderly. Simon's own lips were dry. She was the one. Frankie was the one, probably the only one he was ever truly going to love, and he was going to lose her before he even had her.

"I was thinking about it, yeah. On the other hand, I may just throw up. I suppose I could do both simultaneously. . . ."

"So you love her enough to let her go," Dom said.

"That's real sweet, but give *yourself* a break, pal. Love *yourself* enough to fight for her. Besides, look at her body language. She's not comfortable kissing him. She's not sold on this guy—not yet."

Simon didn't see it. He didn't see discomfort or distance. All he saw was Frankie in someone else's arms.

"Dom, they're calling you from the front desk," Vinnie murmured.

"Don't be a fool, Mr. Hunt," Dominic said as he walked away.

Simon watched as Jazz kissed Frankie again. He stood up, uncertain of what to do. Should he just cut in? Should he tap Jazz on the shoulder mid-kiss? Should he wait until they went back to their table and pull up a neighborly chair?

Or should he stand up on the bar and shout across the room that he loved her? Yeah, that would be incomparable fun. He wasn't sure he'd be able to get the words *I love you* past his lips even in private. It would be much too risky ever to reveal himself that way. It would be emotional hara-kiri. Three little words would rip him asunder, spilling his quivering feelings out naked onto the floor for her to kick aside or walk on.

Simon took a step toward the dance floor. Cut in. He was going to have to cut in.

But before he took another step, Frankie pulled back from Jazz and asked him something. Jazz shrugged and tried to pull her close again, but Frankie resisted. She gestured toward the top pocket of his jacket. Again Jazz shrugged. Frankie gestured again, pulling free from his arms, and Jazz finally took something from his pocket and handed it to Frankie. Frankie looked at it carefully and handed it back to him.

And then, while Simon watched, she hauled back and punched Jazz Chester in the jaw.

Jazz went down onto the dance floor, and a gasp went up from the other restaurant patrons. Frankie turned and made a beeline for the door.

Simon stepped toward her. "Francine . . ."

She didn't hear him, didn't see him. She pushed right past him in her haste to leave the room.

Simon glanced back at Jazz. He'd picked himself up, shaking his head ruefully at the waiters' and maître d's attentive concern. He made no attempt to go after Frankie.

Which was just as well, because Simon followed her, picking up his pace as she headed toward the elevators.

TEN

Frankie closed her eyes and let the elevator carry her up to the fifth floor.

Damn Jazz Chester. Damn him to hell. And as long as she was angry and hurt, she might as well add Simon Hunt's name to the list. Damn Simon too. Damn him for being right, and damn him for not being there now, of all times, when she needed him the most.

Frankie opened her eyes and stared at the numbers lighting up above the elevator door. One more floor. She'd promised herself she wouldn't cry until she made it into her room and locked the door behind her.

But her knuckles on her right hand were bruised and raw from punching Jazz in the face. It was the final blow to both her pride and her psyche—the straw of pain and embarrassment that was trying its hardest to break the camel's back.

Frankie couldn't hold in slightly hysterical-sounding laughter. She'd *punched* Jazz Chester in the *face*. God help her if Simon ever found out. She and Leila had once argued with Simon for hours over the theory that women were superior to men because they reacted to bad news and disappointment by discussing their emotions rather than internalizing or lashing out.

She'd just "discussed" Jazz's face with her fist, and shot *that* theory to hell.

Lord, her hand hurt.

Her heart hurt worse.

The old-fashioned elevator doors opened on the fifth floor, and Frankie stepped out. Her room was around to the left, past the fire stairs and—

The door that led to the stairs burst open, and a man leapt out. Frankie jumped back in alarm and assumed a fighting stance.

But the man didn't move toward her. In fact, he was breathing hard and he leaned back against the wall in a very nonthreatening way. He was blond, like Simon, and tall, like Simon, and . . .

He glanced over at her, taking in her martial arts pose, and laughed. "Lose your frying pan, Francine?"

It was Simon. It was *Simon*? Frankie slowly stood up, staring as he doubled over, hands on his knees, head down.

"Are you all right?" She asked it at the exact same time he did. "Owe me a Coke," he added, still trying to catch his breath. He raked his hair back from his face as he looked up at her from his awkward position.

What was he doing here?

"Stitch in my side from running up five flights of stairs," he explained, still holding his side as he carefully straightened up. "Oh, man, look at your hand. . . . We've got to get some ice for this."

He reached for her bruised hand so gently, with so much concern on his face, that Frankie felt her eyes well with tears. She fought hard to blink them back. "I punched out Jazz," she told him.

Simon didn't seem shocked or appalled or amused or even the least bit surprised. "I know," he said gently. "What happened?"

Frankie shook her head. She couldn't tell him. Not yet.

He led her toward a small room that held a soda machine and an ice maker. "Don't tell me I'm going to have to sneak a look in your diary to find out exactly what he did to get you so mad."

Frankie couldn't talk about it. She couldn't *think* about it. Not until she closed the door of her room. Not until it was safe to cry. She took a deep breath instead. "What are you doing here? I fired you."

He smiled, letting go of her hand as he opened the sliding door to the ice maker. "Here's a hot tip from the Fortune 500 big book of business rules: You can't fire someone who's never been on the payroll in the first place." He looked around for something to hold the ice, but there was nothing—no containers, no plastic bags. He pulled the front tails of his shirt out of his pants.

"But you weren't on the plane." Frankie's voice trembled slightly. Lord, *everything* was a trigger for emotional distress. The day had been fraught with too much disappointment and too little sleep. The combination was crippling.

He glanced down at her, his gaze sharp. "Did you miss me?"

She couldn't answer that—not without giving herself away. She folded her arms across her chest, holding on to herself tightly. "I thought you changed your mind."

"You didn't really think you could scare me off that easily, did you?"

"I thought . . ." Frankie had thought whatever this game was that he was playing with her was of such little importance to him that when something or someone more interesting surfaced, he'd had no problem shrugging her off.

"I missed the flight." Taking the scoop, Simon held out the front of his shirt like a bowl and began filling it with ice. "One of my clients had the audacity to expect me actually to do business and make a sale for them, can you believe it? I had to catch a later plane out of Sarasota." He closed the ice maker's door and straightened up, holding his shirt out slightly from the smooth, tanned muscles of his stomach. He was wearing khaki Dockers, and with his shirt pulled up, the tiny edge of a pair of wildly colored boxer shorts showed.

Frankie forced herself to look anywhere else as he led her down the hall. "How did you know I was staying here?"

"I called Clay Quinn. I'm not a half-bad detective

myself, you know. What's your room number, Francine? My stomach is about to freeze."

"Five sixteen." Simon stopped in front of the door, waiting as Frankie searched her pockets for her key. She glanced up at him as she unlocked the door, feeling oddly shy and extremely volatile, the emotions of the past few hours racing around inside of her, searching for an outlet to be set free. "I still can't believe you're really here."

He tucked a stray lock of hair behind her ear. It was an incredibly sweet and gentle gesture and it made her want to weep. His eyes were so soft, such a warm shade of blue. "I thought you might need me," he said quietly.

It was the kindness of his voice that did her in. She felt herself crumble, her emotions avalanching in on themselves. "I did." She felt the tears she'd held in for so long start to force their way free. She felt her lower lip tremble like a lost child's. "I do. I do need you, Si."

One more step and she'd be inside her room. One more step. But she couldn't make it. She couldn't move. Tears flooded her eyes and escaped down her cheeks as Simon took her arm and pulled her over the threshold.

She heard the door close tightly behind her as she gave in to the tears. She sank down onto the dark pink carpeting, overcome by exhaustion and hurt, barely aware that Simon moved swiftly, vanishing somewhere behind her. She heard the clatter of ice in the bathroom sink as if from a distance, and then he was back, enveloping her in the warmth of his arms, pulling her onto his lap, holding her close right there on the floor.

He didn't question her. He didn't ask for explanations. He just rocked her gently and let her cry.

"I'm here," he whispered. "As long as you need me, Frankie, I'll be here for you."

She felt his hands in her hair, stroking her back—comforting hands, strong hands. It felt so good. When was the last time she'd let herself be taken care of like this? She couldn't remember. Gram had died years before and for the last five years of the old woman's life, Frankie had been the caregiver. She'd been the strong one, always ready to smile or give comfort.

Her college boyfriend, Charlie, had wanted to take care of her. But his idea of providing care meant treating her like a child, taking all decisions out of her hands, making her his responsibility. His touch had been proprietary.

Simon's was not.

With Simon she was an equal. He'd treated her that way even when she *was* a child.

She'd soaked the collar of his shirt. His neck was damp and she wiped at it ineffectively as she lifted her head to look up at him.

His face was somber as he met her gaze. She could see a flash of uncertainty in his eyes, and it unsettled her.

"Hurts bad, huh?" he asked softly.

She nodded, suddenly aware that she was sitting on the floor, on Simon Hunt's lap, with his arms around her. His nose was an inch and a half away from hers, his mouth not much farther.

She could handle irreverent, devil-may-care Simon with his jokes and teasing. It was this other side of him, this quiet, thoughtful, *vulnerable* Simon that she found hard to deal with—and even harder to resist.

"Is there anything I can do to fix it?" he asked.

Frankie shook her head. He smelled like the ocean and fresh air and subtle traces of expensive cologne. It was the way he'd smelled for years, familiar and warm and sweetly delicious. She would have been able to find him in a darkened warehouse with her eyes closed.

"You really . . ." He cleared his throat. "You really care a lot for this guy, huh?"

It took her a moment to realize he was talking about Jazz.

Jazz.

Frankie pulled free from Simon's arms, moving to sit next to him on the floor, her back against the wall. He took her hand, lacing their fingers together.

"You don't have to answer that," he said quietly. "You don't have to tell me anything at all—unless you want to tell me to find him and break the *other* side of his jaw."

She turned to look at him. "You don't really think I broke his jaw, do you?"

Simon picked up her right hand, examining her bruised knuckles. "Can you wiggle your fingers?"

She could and she did. It hurt, but nothing seemed to be broken. She glanced up at him again.

He smiled slightly. "I'd be willing to bet since your hand's not broken, his jaw's not either."

"Too bad."

Simon shook his head. "He's an idiot. There's got to be something seriously wrong with him."

It was Frankie's turn to laugh, but there was no humor in her voice. "You know, I thought it was going to be the way you predicted—that my expectations of Jazz wouldn't stand up to the real man, but . . . I was wrong. You were wrong. He was everything I remembered. And more. He met me in the lobby with a single rose. While we were waiting for our drinks, we had a conversation in which he actually recited several lines of poetry." She laughed again. "He's smart, successful, romantic, handsome, *sensitive*. . . . He's *perfect*."

Simon looked away, his attention seemingly captured by the sight of their hands clasped together. He loosened his grip, as if suddenly aware he was squeezing her hand too tightly. "And that was why you punched him? Because he's perfect?"

"He asked me to dance," Frankie told him. "So there we were, on the dance floor, and yes, it was perfect. It was romantic. He didn't even mind that I was wearing jeans."

"Famous movie stars can get away with that."

She looked at him sharply. "How did you know . . . ?"

"Me and Vinnie, the bartender, go way back."

"You were *there*?"

"I saw you dancing." Simon's gaze shifted to her mouth. "I saw him kiss you. That looked pretty damned perfect to me too."

Frankie felt her cheeks start to heat. She couldn't believe she was sitting there, talking to Simon about kissing Jazz. "Like I said, Jazz hasn't changed."

"Then I saw you have what looked like an argument."

Frankie nodded. "It was the weirdest thing." She turned toward him, suddenly wanting to tell him, needing *some*one to know. "We were dancing, right? He had my right hand in his left." Simon nodded. "He . . . kissed me, and yes, it *was* perfect. I mean . . ." She shrugged. "It was *perfect*. He looked in my eyes, and he smiled, as if we were sharing some kind of secret, as if he knew that that kiss rated in the decade's top-ten list of most romantic events, and he pulled me in closer and pressed my hand over his heart. I swear, the guy was oozing romance."

Simon didn't say a word. He just waited for her to continue.

"That's when I felt it." Frankie shook her head, still amazed at the turn of events. It was only chance that she found out. Otherwise, she never would have known. . . .

Simon didn't have a clue what she was talking about. *That's when I felt it.* She could tell from his face that he was imagining in the entirely wrong direction.

"He had a ring in the breast pocket of his jacket," she explained.

He still didn't get it.

"A plain band," she continued.

Simon's eyebrows flickered as he frowned slightly.

"I was dancing with Jazz," Frankie went on, "and I looked down at his left hand, and there was a pale stripe on his ring finger. Now, that's not so strange—he told me his marriage had ended not too long ago. But I couldn't keep from wondering why a recently divorced man would keep his *wedding* ring in the breast pocket of his jacket."

A lightbulb went on over Simon's head. "You mean . . . ?"

"He's not divorced. He's not even separated. He's married. Jazz Chester is a smart, successful, romantic, handsome, sensitive, lying, cheating bastard." Frankie looked down at her bruised knuckles. "So I hit him."

Her eyes filled with tears again. Lord, who would've thought she had any tears left?

"Frankie, I'm sorry," Simon said quietly.

Blinking hard, she looked up at him, trying her best to smile. "Why? You called it, remember?" She shook her head. "God, he *lied* to me. Well . . . no, actually, he didn't *lie*. He never actually *said* he was divorced, he let me assume it and didn't tell me otherwise."

She looked back at her sore hand, tried to flex her fingers, and winced. Simon stood up. "Let me wrap some ice in a towel."

Frankie's legs ached as she, too, pushed herself up off the floor. "You know what bothers me the most?" she asked, following him into the bathroom.

He shook his head no, watching her in the mirror that covered one entire wall of the big white-tiled room as he folded some ice into a hand towel. Big? This room was larger than her living room. Two sinks were set into a long counter that spanned one side of the room. A Jacuzzi tub was built into the wall across from it. Over in the other corner was a shower stall large enough for a basketball team.

Frankie sat down on the edge of the tub, bringing her attention back to Simon. He looked nearly as tired as she felt. His hair was tousled and his shirt was cried on, sleeves rolled up and tails untucked. His pants were wrinkled and he'd kicked off his shoes and peeled off his socks at some point in the evening—probably since they'd returned to her room.

He looked like a man who was getting ready to go to bed. Frankie had to look away, afraid that what she was thinking would show in her eyes. She was afraid that he'd somehow know that as she was dancing with Jazz Chester tonight, she'd been wishing she were with him instead. The truth was, even if Jazz *had* been perfect, she wouldn't have gone home with him. How could she start a relationship with one man when she couldn't stop thinking about another?

Simon sat next to her on the rim of the tub. He lifted her bruised hand and wrapped the towel and ice around it. "Sorry," he murmured when she drew in a short breath of pain. "Tell me. What bothers you the most?"

"It's just that . . . it worked out so perfectly in theory. Me and Jazz, I mean. Talk about destiny—we meet again after all these years . . . To end up with the boy I first loved—the boy who gave me my first kiss. Could it have been any more romantic?"

Her question was rhetorical, but Simon considered it thoughtfully. "Well, yeah, I could think of one or two scenarios—"

"But that's not the part that really bothers me," she said. "What bothers me is the fact that now all my memories are tainted."

"Tainted."

She glanced up at him, but there wasn't any amusement in his eyes. Only puzzlement. He was truly trying to follow her, trying to understand.

"I had a first kiss that was like something from a romance novel." She smiled sadly, remembering. "It was an incredible night—one of those warm spring nights on the key, where the air smells like tropical flowers and the stars look close enough to reach out and touch. A breeze was coming in off the Gulf, but it was from the south, and it was warm. We were on the beach, in the moonlight, with the sound of the surf . . ." She shook her head. "It was . . . right out of a movie. We were walking and Jazz took my hand and I was nervous as hell." Nearly as nervous as she was sitting there with Simon's leg pressed comfortably against hers, with his eyes glued to her face, listening to her story as intently as if she were telling him the secret to eternal life. "We'd been on the beach hanging with the same crowd of kids all day, and I'd flirted with him most of that time, but finally we were alone. He stopped walking, and he just looked at me, and I was so sure I could see all the way into his soul just from looking in his eyes. And then he kissed me. It was perfect."

She risked another glance in Simon's direction. "But Jazz was probably as insincere then as he is now. That kiss was just a fake."

"You don't know that for sure."

"Yeah, but now I'll always wonder," she said. "I know this sounds stupid, but I feel really ripped off. See, it's not as if I can go back and do it over again. I mean, you get only one shot at something like a first kiss, and I blew mine by kissing a jerk."

Simon was silent, and when Frankie looked at him again, she caught another glimpse of that unsettling vulnerability in his eyes. "Maybe you're wrong. Maybe Jazz *wasn't* the first boy you kissed."

"I think I probably would remember—"

"You were twelve," Simon said. "You wrote about it in your diary."

"What?" She glanced up at him, frowning. "Who . . . ?"

"You kissed *me*, Francine."

The look in his eyes hadn't changed, and Frankie felt hypnotized. She couldn't look away. Her pulse kicked into double time and she felt light-headed. "That was just make-believe."

"You wrote about it as if it were real."

"I wish it had been," Frankie whispered. At least then she'd know he'd meant it. If nothing else, Simon was sincere in his affairs. He lived for the moment, and for that moment he meant and felt what he said.

For the first time in what had seemed like an eternity, Simon smiled. "Really?" He didn't wait for an answer. He stood up, taking the towel and ice away from her hand and dumping them into the sink. "Maybe it *was* real and we just don't remember. Or . . . or maybe it was *supposed* to be real, and we got sidetracked. Maybe that kiss with Jazz Chester was just practice. Maybe Charlie and everyone else you've ever kissed, maybe that was all just practice for the real thing."

The real thing? As Frankie stared at him in shock, Simon turned on the overhead heat lamp and switched off the bright vanity lights. The room was dimmer with only the reddish-orange glow. It was warmer too. "You wrote in your diary that it was evening. It was early summer—muggy and hot."

Simon started unbuttoning his shirt, but then gave up and just pulled it over his head. "I was with all the guys, and we were coming out of the rec center gym after a basketball game. My shirt was off. You wrote that I had a towel around my neck." He took a towel from the rack and placed it just so.

"I was limping," he continued. "I twisted my ankle in the game, and it hurt, so I was standing off to the side, away from the others." He reached down and took her hand, pulling her up so that she was standing beside him. She could feel the warmth from the heat lamp beating down on her head, but it was nothing compared to the heat she felt from the touch of Simon's hand.

"You came over and asked if I was all right." His

voice was husky as he looked down at her. "You asked if I needed any help walking home. I smiled and thanked you, and told you that Bob or Davey would help me out. But I couldn't get their attention. They were flirting with Jenny Brooks or someone, so you put your arm around my waist. . . ."

He did just that and Frankie drew in a deep breath at the sensation of her bare arm against the smooth, warm skin of his back.

"And I put my arm around your shoulder and used you as a crutch."

"Simon—"

He put his finger on her lips. "Shh. Work with me here, okay, Francine?" He pulled her with him into the corner of the room, opening the door to the big shower stall and stepping inside.

"Si—"

"That's when it started to rain," he told her, reaching forward and turning on the shower.

"Simon!" Frankie sputtered as warm water hit her directly in the face.

"All my friends ran for home." Simon held her tightly so she couldn't get away. "Everyone but you. You stayed there with me, getting soaked, because you knew I couldn't run with my ankle hurt the way it was."

Frankie couldn't keep from laughing. They were standing there, in the shower, with their clothes on, enacting a twelve-year-old's fantasy. It was too absurd.

Or was it?

Water was streaming down Simon's face as he

reached forward to push back her wet hair. His eyes were so warm as he gazed at her, Frankie's heart nearly stopped. He was going to kiss her.

"For a twelve-year-old, you were pretty astute," he murmured. "Standing in the rain is incredibly romantic, don't you think? It washes everything unimportant away. You don't stand in the rain for small talk, you know?"

Frankie nodded.

"So we're standing there, drenched, and you look into my eyes, and you know this is it. I'm going to kiss you." His voice dropped. "And then I do."

Slowly, he lowered his head, stopping a fraction of an inch from her lips, hesitating. He held her gaze, searching her eyes, for the first time really letting her have a good long look at his uncertainty, his vulnerability. He was scared. Frankie saw that this kiss meant something to him, and he was scared that she'd push him away, and equally scared that she *wouldn't*.

And just like that, Frankie fell. Headlong, she fell into the bottomless blue depths of his eyes. She was swallowed up, engulfed by his heat, by the complicated warmth of his soul.

And she lifted her chin that extra fraction of an inch and kissed him, lightly brushing her lips across his.

It was all the encouragement he needed. He reached up and cupped her face with his hands and gently, sweetly, claimed her lips with his own.

It wasn't the kind of kiss she'd expected from Simon. It was so soft, so tender. He kissed her again, deeper this time, and her insides melted.

He tasted warm and sweet and so incredibly wonderful. And Frankie wanted more. She put her arms up around his neck, and he responded instantly, pulling her closer as the water from the shower pounded down around them.

And now his kiss was laced with fire. He kissed her again and again, harder, deeper, leaving her breathless and dizzy. His hands were in her hair, sliding down her back, pressing her hips against him. She could feel his arousal, taste his need.

But he pulled back, out of breath, groaning and laughing. He turned the knob that controlled the temperature of the shower, sending an icy blast of water down on top of them. "You were only twelve," he gasped, turning his face to the water, letting it flow over him, cooling him. "Jeez, I don't think you wrote it *quite* like that."

Frankie reached across him and turned off the water. In the sudden silence she could hear Simon trying hard to steady his breathing. "I'm not twelve anymore," she said, trying her best to sound matter-of-fact, but unable to hide the shaking in her voice. "If I were writing it today, I wouldn't have ended it there."

Simon turned and looked at her. The water from his hair was dripping down onto his nose, but he ignored it. His full attention was focused on her.

Frankie became suddenly self-conscious. Her T-shirt was wet and glued to her body, leaving close to nothing to the imagination.

"How *would* you end it?" he asked.

With a wedding ceremony and a lifetime of happily-ever-after. But she couldn't tell him that. That wasn't what he wanted to hear. This was Simon. No-strings, live-for-the-moment Simon. But the sweet fire of his kisses had given her respite from her hurt and disappointment, leaving this burning anticipation.

She wanted more.

She felt a flare of remorse for their friendship—would it survive a night of passion? She didn't know. She didn't care. She knew only what she'd suspected earlier that evening, when she was dancing with Jazz. She was falling in love with Simon Hunt.

"I'll tell you how I'd end it," Simon continued when she didn't move, didn't speak. His eyes were molten lava, but he hadn't reached for her. He, too, hadn't moved at all. His face looked almost predatory in the reddish glow from the heat lamp. The light glistened on the smooth, wet plains of his chest. He looked savage and dangerous—sheer desire in a human form. "I'd take you home. And I'd help you out of your wet clothes."

Frankie could barely stand, dizzy from the image his words conjured up. Yes, she wanted to say. *Yes.* But she couldn't, not when he looked so intense. She needed to see him smile.

"With your teeth?" she asked him. "Because if *I* were writing it, I'd definitely have you take off my clothes with your teeth."

Simon laughed—a quick, loud bark of humor—a

grin exploding on his face. But it didn't douse the heat in his eyes. In fact, it made it burn hotter, brighter. But still he didn't move toward her. "That works really well for me too."

"You'd carry me to the bed," Frankie told him.

"And I'd kiss you. All over. Starting with your mouth and slowly working my way down."

Frankie shivered. *Yes.* "But meanwhile, I'd have succeeded in taking off *your* clothes too."

"With *your* teeth."

They stood in the shower stall, grinning at each other. Frankie's heart was pounding so loudly, she was sure Simon could hear it. She could see the hunger in his eyes, on his face, in every muscle of his body. He was breathing hard and fast, but still he didn't move.

"I'm not sure what I'm waiting for," he admitted, moistening dry lips with his tongue.

"Some kind of sign from God?"

And then the timer on the heat lamp clicked off, plunging them into near darkness.

ELEVEN

Simon laughed softly, trying to steady his racing heart.

He could see Frankie in the dim light that came through the door. She was watching him, her wet clothes plastered to her body, her dark eyes wide, waiting. He didn't need a sign from God. He needed her reassurance that this was, indeed, what she wanted to do. And to get that, all he really had to do was ask.

"Francine . . ." His voice was husky, so he stopped and cleared his throat. "Do you want—"

"Yes."

Yes. *Yes.* He briefly closed his eyes in a silent prayer of thanks. He was going to make love to Frankie. It was actually going to happen. Right there. Right then.

He took a step toward her, reaching, and she met him halfway. Then she was in his arms, kissing him as fiercely as he kissed her. He was giddy with anticipation, delirious with expectation.

I love you. The words caught in his throat, so he

tried to show her instead, with his hands, with his mouth, with his entire being.

She felt so perfect in his arms. He was tall and she was not, but his arms fit around her exactly, her body molding to his as if she'd been made with him in mind.

Her mouth was sweet and hot and he drank her in eagerly, her tongue engaging his in a dance so sensuous and erotic, he nearly lost his balance.

He tugged at her T-shirt and she helped him pull it up and over her head. He used his teeth to drag the strap of her bra down one shoulder and she laughed aloud and unfastened the front clasp.

Simon couldn't breathe. She was gorgeous. Her breasts were full and round, their darkened tips hardened into tight peaks. He wanted to freeze his surging desire. He wanted to temporarily rein in the waves of his need, to hold himself still, so he could simply gaze at her, so he could step back and take his time and just *look* at Frankie's beautiful body.

But he couldn't keep himself from touching her, from caressing her heart-stoppingly smooth skin, from pressing his face against her soft flesh. He drew one pebble-hard nipple into his mouth, pulling, sucking, laving her with his tongue until she cried out.

He felt her hands on the buckle of his belt, and he knew that the pleasures that awaited him were ones he'd never before known. And that was strange, considering.

In the past, making love to a woman had been purely about pleasure. *His* pleasure. Of course he gave as good as he got, but in the end it was all about his own satisfaction.

But not this time. With Frankie, all bets were off, all rules were rewritten. He wanted to make love with her not merely to quench the thirst of his desire, but to express his emotions, to give voice to these strange and frightening feelings he was experiencing.

He loved her intensely, completely, unswervingly. And he wanted her to know it.

He pushed down her jeans even as he felt her slender fingers unzip his pants. The wet denim clung to her legs, and he laughed his frustration as he knelt down and peeled it from her, pulling her sodden boots from her feet.

Her fingers were in his hair and he looked up at her as she stood finally naked before him. And again, like before, it wasn't enough to look, he had to touch. He pressed his face against the soft smoothness of her belly, sliding his hands over her breasts, her back, her thighs, between her thighs.

"Simon . . ." His name escaped from her lips on a sigh as he touched her most intimately, seeking and finding her wet heat.

He lowered his head, exploring with his lips and tongue where his hands had been. He felt her tense, felt her fingers tighten in his hair, then felt her open herself to him and pull him closer.

He felt her trembling, heard her soft cries, saw her head thrown back in sheer uninhibited pleasure.

He'd died and gone to heaven.

He could feel the tension building in her, sense

how close she was to the brink of release, yet before she reached it, she pulled away.

He couldn't believe it. "Don't you want . . . ?"

She pulled him up, capturing his mouth in a searing kiss as she ineffectively sought to rid him of his own clothes. He kicked his pants and shorts free as she reached for him, closing her fingers around him. "This is what I want."

Yes. He could certainly arrange for her to have that, along with his heart and soul. . . .

"Do you have protection?"

He nodded. Man, he'd been reduced to a speechless idiot. "Somewhere, yeah," he managed to say. His wallet. It was still in the back pocket of his pants, in a tangle on the floor. He spilled his credit cards in his haste to find the condom he carried in among his dollar bills. "Got it." He tore open the paper, and quickly, expertly, covered himself.

She took his hand, pulling him out of the shower stall, toward the bathroom door. But he stopped her.

"Isn't this where I'm supposed to carry you to the bed?"

Frankie laughed. He loved the sound of her laughter.

"Can you do it at a dead run?" she asked, entangling one of her legs with one of his, pressing his arousal against her stomach as she stood on tiptoe to kiss him.

The last of his control vanished under the power of that kiss. He lifted her up, wrapped those gorgeous legs around his waist, and drove himself deeply inside her.

"Yes . . ." They breathed the word at the same time, and Simon lifted his head to look into Frankie's midnight eyes.

"Aren't you gonna say 'owe me a Coke'?" she whispered.

Simon laughed. "No," he said, and kissed her hard.

She returned his kiss voraciously, and began to move on top of him in a way that made his head spin. It was too much, too soon, and he groaned, trying to hold her still, trying desperately to regain his equilibrium. But she didn't want to stop, and truth be told, he didn't want her to either.

But, dear God, they weren't even going to make it out of the bathroom. Determined to achieve at least *that* much dignity, Simon kicked open the bathroom door and propelled them out into the hotel room.

The enormous bed seemed at least as far away as the moon. He'd imagined them making love for the first time on a bed like that, savoring each languorous touch, each deliberate, sensuous caress. He'd imagined taking hours and hours and *hours*, lazily exploring every inch of her body, fully experiencing each delicious sensation, each exquisite moment of ecstasy.

But he seriously doubted his ability to make it over to the bed. Dammit, he was going to disappoint her. Dammit, he was going to—

"I love this," Frankie breathed into his ear. "I love

it hard and fast and deep—like you're gonna die if you can't get enough of me."

Who the hell needed a bed anyway? Making love on a bed was *way* overrated.

Simon turned, pinning her against the wall for leverage. She was sexy as hell with her head thrown back, her breasts slick and gleaming with perspiration. She opened eyes that were dark with passion. "I love this," she whispered again.

I love you. With her anchored firmly against the wall, he was in charge now, but it was tenuous at best. Still, he controlled each stroke, each movement, watching her face, the incredible sensations he was feeling amplified a thousand times over by her obvious pleasure.

It couldn't get any better. It couldn't, but then it did. Frankie opened her eyes again. "Oh, Simon," she breathed. His name sounded like music when she said it that way. As she held his gaze, he felt the beginnings of her release, and she smiled.

It was the same smile she'd given him when he'd won the free-throw contest the year before he'd graduated from college. It was the same smile she'd given him when he'd made his first major antiques deal. It was the smile she'd given him when Leila and Marsh had announced their wedding engagement.

It was a smile of pure joy. It was pure Frankie. And it pushed him over the edge.

He held her gaze as he felt himself explode, felt his own lips curve up into an answering smile even as his body and brain shattered into a million scorching, ecstatic pieces. He felt himself shake, felt her grip him tightly, heard himself cry out, heard her whisper his name again and again as he rocketed light-years outside of previously explored space, into new, uncharted territory.

Stupidity.

Frankie had done a number of stupid things in her life, but waking up in Simon Hunt's arms was an entirely new study in stupidity.

She lay in the predawn light, hardly daring to breathe for fear of waking him. But he was sound asleep, one arm thrown possessively across her. His hair was rumpled and he needed a shave, but despite that, he was entirely too handsome. His eyelashes looked to be about four miles long against his smooth, tanned cheeks. His elegant lips were slightly upturned in a contented smile. He looked boyish and innocent—of which he was neither.

Of course, she herself wouldn't quite fit in the innocent category anymore. Certainly not after last night . . .

After their first incredible round of lovemaking, they'd fallen into bed and slept for many hours. But Frankie had woken in the night and, as if in some wild, erotic dream, she in turn had woken Simon with her hands and her mouth and her tongue. Somehow they'd ended up on the floor, in an exchange of passion no less tempestuous than their first steamy encounter.

And now, here she was, staring at the eggshell-fine cracks in the elegant old hotel ceiling in the early morning light, miserable as hell.

She was a fool for making love to Simon. Yes, he was hard to resist, but resisting him was not impossible. She'd been resisting him for years. But now she was no longer content with her life because she'd had a taste of what it would be like to have Simon as a permanent, full-time lover.

And she knew damn well that the words *permanent* and *full-time* weren't in Simon's vocabulary.

Yes, she was a fool. She'd sampled the forbidden fruit, and now she was forced to see the truth she'd been hiding from herself for God only knows how many years.

She loved Simon.

It was sheer stupidity, because she could never, ever have him. Not for more than the fleeting few weeks that his affairs usually lasted. She knew she couldn't change him—she'd seen far too many women try to do that and fail. She was wise enough not to make that same mistake. She was smart enough to keep at least *that* much of her dignity.

Still, she was in love with the man. She'd been forced to admit it. She couldn't deny it any longer. And now she was going to have to live with that, probably for the rest of her life.

Although the pain of living with that knowledge was going to be a million times easier to handle than watching the desire in his eyes turn into that trapped look he always got a few weeks into a relationship.

And *that* pain was nothing compared to the awful thought of his finding out her true feelings.

And he *would* find out. If he so much as kissed her again, he'd see the love in her eyes.

And then she'd see nothing but pity and fear in *his* eyes.

It was too awful to consider.

It was not, however, unavoidable.

Soundlessly, she slipped out of bed and went into the bathroom, taking her suitcase and locking the door behind her.

Ecstasy.

It wasn't something that Simon had experienced frequently in his life.

At least not before last night.

He woke up smiling, remembering, reliving. He rolled over, hoping to find Frankie somewhere on one of the outer acres of the oversized bed, but came up empty-handed.

She wasn't there.

He sat up, alarmed, but sank back down, hearing the sound of the water running in the bathroom.

He had to laugh at himself. For one panicked moment he'd imagined that she'd woken up early and sneaked out of the room. But that was ridiculous. This was *her* room. Besides, *he* was the one with the reputation for sneaking away after sexual encounters. And this time he wasn't going anywhere.

He was in love with Frankie Paresky.

So why hadn't he told her? *I love you.* Three easy words. Easy to pronounce. Not a tongue twister.

He'd had plenty of opportunities. Such as when she woke him in the middle of the night . . .

Simon closed his eyes, reveling in the remembered ecstasy, feeling his morning arousal growing. After last night, he was amazed that he'd been celibate by choice for all those months. After last night, he was amazed that he'd known Frankie for close to twenty years, and yet he'd had no idea just how incredible making love to her could be.

He listened to the noises in the bathroom, hoping for the sound of the shower. If Frankie turned on the shower, he'd get up, join her in there. . . .

But the shower didn't go on. Instead, he heard the sound of a hair dryer. Was it really possible that she was done with her shower, and was already drying her hair? Simon turned to look at the clock on the television set. Seven A.M. Man, she must have been up early to be already showered by seven A.M.

God, was Frankie a morning person? He definitely was not. That was going to take some getting used to. The thought was a little frightening. . . .

Frightening.

There was more to this that was frightening than whether or not Frankie was a morning person. And that, Simon suddenly realized, was the real reason he hadn't been able to tell Frankie that he loved her.

He was scared to death. Ecstatic, but scared to death all the same.

He'd never felt like this before. He thought it was

love. It *had* to be love. But what if everything he was feeling just up and disappeared? What if it faded? What if he was wrong and this burning sensation in his chest proved to be nothing but indigestion?

And what if he made a promise that he couldn't keep?

The sound of the hair dryer stopped, but Frankie still didn't come out of the bathroom. What was she doing in there?

Simon threw back the covers and got out of bed.

He padded, naked, over to the bathroom door and knocked. "Hey, Francine?"

There was only silence from inside the bathroom.

He knocked again. "Are you okay in there?"

The bathroom door opened. Frankie. She was wearing a man's red cotton button-down shirt over a pair of jeans. She looked beautiful. Her hair was still a bit damp, and she smelled clean and fresh. Simon felt himself smile just at the sight of her.

"Good morning." He reached for her, wanting to feel her body next to his, but she stepped away.

"I left your clothes out by the bed." She folded her arms across her chest and leaned back against the bathroom counter. "I thought you'd be gone by now."

Simon heard her words but couldn't make any sense of them. "Gone?" What the hell was she talking about? The first thin blade of fear penetrated his heart. He reached for her again, and again she anticipated his move and slid farther down the counter, away from him. Something was wrong.

She gazed down at the floor, as if she were afraid even to look in his direction. "I guess we have to talk."

"Okay. I'm listening."

She glanced up at him, then quickly away, looking back down at the floor. "Simon, you're naked."

"Yeah, I was naked last night too." He kept his voice light, teasing. He even managed to smile. "You didn't seem to mind it then."

He'd meant it as a joke, but she didn't react at all. Something was *very* wrong here. His fear sharpened.

"Would you please get dressed so we can talk?"

Simon kept his voice even. "You mind if I, um, use the bathroom first?"

She shook her head and vanished, closing the door behind her.

Simon relieved himself, then washed his hands, staring at his face in the mirror. What the hell had he done wrong? It was clear this talk was going to be all bad news, but he couldn't for the life of him figure out why.

He splashed water onto his face. Whatever it was, it was a mistake, a misunderstanding. They'd talk, he'd clear it up, they'd order room service, and he'd sweet-talk her back into bed before the coffee was cool.

He hoped.

He dried his face on a towel and opened the bathroom door.

His clothes were in a neat little pile right outside the door. Hint, hint.

His boxer shorts and pants were still a little damp,

but he pulled them on anyway. He didn't bother buttoning his shirt before he went out into the room.

Frankie was sitting at a small table, sorting through one of the boxes from Jazz's mother's desk. She didn't look up until he sat down across from her.

Her face was expressionless. The night before he'd been able to read every look, every smile, every movement of her face perfectly. But now all he could see was . . . nothing.

He took a deep breath. "Talk to me."

She looked up, steadily meeting his gaze with eyes that carefully guarded her every secret. "I just wanted to thank you for last night."

She wanted to *what*? Again, it was as if she were speaking a foreign language. Simon leaned forward. "Come again?"

"Thank you," she repeated. "Last night was . . . fun."

Fun? *Fun*? Simon was speechless. Last night had been soul-shattering, not *fun*. Bowling was *fun*.

"I just wanted to tell you that, you know, you don't have to worry. I, uh—" She hesitated, clearing her throat and pushing her hair back from her face.

Horseback riding on the beach was *fun*. A barbecue with friends was *fun*. As Simon gazed at her, she seemed to collect herself and continue.

"I know what we shared was only a one-night stand, and . . ." She smiled, but it was nothing like the smiles she'd given him the night before. "I'm okay with that. I knew that before this whole affair started, and that's good, that's all that I wanted. I mean, we got it all out of our systems, right? Now everything can just go back to normal."

Going to the movies was *fun*. Casual sex was *fun*.

Simon was stunned. He'd had an incredible night of ecstasy, and she'd had a fun night of casual sex.

Normal. One-night stand. Out of our systems. Her words echoed in his mind. How many times in the past had he thought or felt or even said similar things? He didn't much like hearing those words now.

"A one-night stand," he repeated slowly, choosing each word carefully, afraid he'd slip and give himself away. "Don't you want . . . something more than that, Francine?"

"No." She didn't hesitate before she spoke, and again she held his gaze steadily, forcefully. Coldly. "I don't. I'm not—I never was—interested in anything more from you than friendship, Si. You know that."

I love you. Simon's teeth were clenched as he nodded. "I see." He couldn't tell her now—God, how could he?

Frankie went back to work, quietly sorting through stacks of papers and files.

Simon was at a total loss. What was it that friends did, exactly, after a night of fun casual sex? Did they order breakfast? Read the morning paper?

Or did they do what he always did, and slink back to their rooms alone, aware that the togetherness of the previous night hadn't been real, that it was only a nebulous illusion they'd temporarily pretended had substance and worth?

Simon stood up.

Or did they drop to their knees, burying their faces in their lover's laps, begging them to reconsider, baring their broken hearts and shattered souls as they proclaimed their undying love?

He'd been on the receiving end of *that* before and hadn't much liked it either.

"I'm going to my room to shower," he told Frankie quietly.

She barely even glanced up. "Okay."

"Call me if you . . . need me. I'm in Room 765."

"Okay. I think I've got this under control though. Thanks."

Thanks. Simon picked up his shoes and socks from where he'd left them the night before. He looked back at Frankie, but she hadn't looked up.

Thanks. He checked to make sure his wallet and his room key were in his pocket, then looked back at Frankie again. She still hadn't even moved.

Thanks. He unlocked the door and turned the knob, and looked back at Frankie one last time. Nothing. Not so much as a glance.

Simon let himself out and closed the door behind him, checking to see that it was locked. Slowly he walked around the corner to the elevator, totally, thoroughly numb.

Inside the room, Frankie dropped her head onto her folded arms and wept.

TWELVE

Frankie sat on the very edge of the bed as she waited for Bradford Quinn to pick up his phone. Clay Quinn had been out of his office. He was in court all day, his secretary had told Frankie. He wouldn't be back until well after seven tonight, and probably wouldn't even have time to phone in to the office for messages before then. But did she want to leave a message anyway?

Frankie had left John Marshall's phone number and address, and the news that she'd actually spoken to the man, who indeed appeared to be Alice Winfield's old and trusted friend. She'd told the secretary to tell Mr. Quinn that she was going to call his brother with the same information.

Now she sat staring at the thick piece of linen-blend paper upon which Clay had jotted his brother's name and phone number, trying not to let herself be aware that the night before she'd shared this bed she was sitting on with Simon Hunt.

He was a fabulous lover.

Of course, she hadn't expected anything else. Lord knows, he'd had years and years of practice.

She wearily rested her head in the palm of her hand, wishing she'd had the strength to allow herself to enjoy the pleasure of Simon's company for a little bit longer. But she didn't.

He'd hardly batted an eye when she fed him that "it was only a one-night stand" nonsense. And if he looked at all perturbed, it was probably because she'd stolen his lines, damn him.

"Ms. Paresky? This is Brad Quinn. Sorry to keep you waiting." The voice on the line was deep and rich and familiar.

"You sound a lot like your brother," Frankie told him.

"Same genes," he said easily. "We look alike too. Both cute as hell."

"Who's older?" She couldn't resist asking.

"He is. By about ten years. I assume you're calling for a reason?"

"I found your aunt Alice's friend John."

"Glory allelu! We've got taxes coming due, and everyone benefits by settling the will ASAP," Brad said. "Okay, I've got a paper and pen. Hit me with the details."

Frankie quickly filled him in.

"You've made Clay and me very happy men," Brad told her. "Our best-case scenario didn't have you finding John Marshall for another week and a half."

"The promise of a cash bonus was added incentive."

He chuckled. "I bet. We'll just need to verify Marshall's identity, and then we'll wire those funds directly to your bank. Send your bank information along with the invoice for your services.

"I will."

"Oh, as long as I've got you on the phone," Brad said, "maybe you could help me out. According to Alice's will, she's left me—personally—the contents of that house down on Sunrise Key."

Frankie sat up in surprise, trying to recall her conversations with Clay Quinn. She'd assumed that when he'd told her about the property on Pelican Street being left to John Marshall, that the contents of the house were included. Obviously, she'd been wrong.

"I don't have time to go down to Florida right now, and I was wondering if you knew someone on the island who might be able to estimate the value—if there even is any—of the furniture in the house?"

"Are you looking to sell it?" she asked.

"Definitely," he said. "And I guess I'll also need to make arrangements for someone to remove and dispose of all of Alice's personal belongings."

"I'd be happy to take care of that for you. Are you sure there's nothing there that you or your relatives would want? I know Alice kept extensive photo albums. . . ."

"To be honest, I didn't know her that well," Brad admitted. "And as far as your taking care of her personal effects, of course I'll pay you for your time."

"She was a friend of mine, Mr. Quinn," Frankie said quietly.

"But I insist. It's still going to take up quite a few of your workdays," he replied. "And if you can think of anyone who can take a look at that furniture—"

"Simon Hunt." Frankie felt her heart ache just from speaking his name. "He's our local antiques dealer. I'll have him give you a call this afternoon."

"Perfect," Brad Quinn said. "Oh, and, Ms. Paresky—good job."

Frankie hung up the phone, feeling nothing. Good job. Yeah, she'd done a good job, but she felt no pride, no sense of fulfillment. She felt no excitement about the ten-thousand-dollar bonus that would arrive in a matter of weeks. She felt nothing but emptiness.

She missed Simon desperately.

"Concierge. May I help you?"

"Dom, is that you?" The voice on the other end of the telephone could have been Dominic Defeo's, but with that purebred accent, Simon wasn't quite sure.

"It is, sir."

"It's me, Simon Hunt."

"Ah. And how did your evening go?"

Simon was silent. At the time, he'd thought it had gone great. But not anymore.

Dominic read his silence correctly. "Yes," he said, "I thought as much." His voice got lower, whispery, and the high-society accent disappeared. "Your lady friend is standing not three feet away from me at the front desk—checking out of the hotel. Without you, pal."

Simon swore sharply. *"Now?"*

"Indeed, sir," he said full voice, the accent firmly back in place. "I suggest you take action immediately."

Simon was already pulling on his shoes. "I'm on my way. Stall her for me, Dom, please?"

"I assure you, sir, I'll do everything in my power to do just that."

"Bless you."

Simon stuffed his still-damp pants and shorts into his overnight bag, gathered his toothbrush and razor from the bathroom, grabbed his jacket from where he'd thrown it on back of a chair, and was out the door in a flash.

The elevator going down moved hellishly slowly, but he forced himself not to run as he stepped out into the lobby and headed toward the front desk. If Frankie was going to believe this was a chance meeting, he couldn't look as if he were chasing her.

There she was.

She was standing at the desk, travel bag over one shoulder, glancing impatiently at her watch. Dominic looked up and caught Simon's eyes, sending a silent message. *Hurry.*

But Simon stopped to buy a paper at the newsstand. He opened it and pretended to be engrossed in the headlines as he stood in line at the hotel's front desk, waiting for the next available clerk to assist him.

"The itemized receipt of your long-distance

charges will be coming shortly," he heard Dom tell Frankie. "I appreciate your patience." He turned toward Simon. "In the meantime, may I help *you*, sir?"

Simon folded the newspaper in half and stepped up to the counter, placing his key on its shiny surface. "I'd like to check out."

He sensed more than saw Frankie stiffen. She saw him. She knew he was there.

He turned toward her slowly, then did a double take as if he were surprised to see her. "Hey." He forced himself to relax, to smile, to play it cool as he leaned back on one elbow on the hotel's front desk.

She nodded once, looking away, and Simon felt a stab of pain. How could she act so cold, so detached? Man, the things they'd done and the heat they'd created together the night before had been off the scale. How could she make love to him like that and then turn around and feel *nothing* in the morning?

What was he doing here? Why was he even bothering to try to change her mind? Clearly, it was a losing battle. . . .

Dominic placed a form on the counter in front of Frankie and handed her a pen. "One more signature, please, madam."

She picked up the pen and dropped it.

That was when Simon saw her hands.

They were shaking.

Whatever she was feeling, it wasn't the nothing that she'd carefully pasted onto her face.

It was enough to give him hope.

"What time does your flight leave?" he asked.

She looked up as if she were surprised, as if she'd forgotten he was standing there. "Oh," she said. "A little bit after one."

"Mine too," Simon lied. He didn't even have a ticket. But he was going to be on that one o'clock flight to Florida if it was the last thing he did. He smiled at her. "Great. We can share a cab to the airport."

A flash of panic filled her eyes as she stared at him, and again he felt a surge of hope. He could almost see the wheels turning in her head as she considered and rejected all the ways she might possibly turn down his offer. But she could find no plausible reason why they *shouldn't* share a cab.

"Congratulations," Simon said. "Am I right to congratulate you? Did you find John Marshall?"

Frankie nodded. "I also found out that Clay Quinn's brother, Bradford, was bequeathed the contents of the Pelican Street house. He wants to sell everything—I told him you'd give him a call."

He pulled her into his arms. "That's fabulous news, Francine." She held herself stiffly, away from him, but when he brushed his lips across her cheek, he felt her tremble. He looked down, and for one heart-stopping second he saw an echo of last night's molten heat in her eyes.

He wanted to hold her even closer, to cover her lips with his own and kiss her until she melted, until she couldn't deny that what they'd experienced had been life-changing. But she pulled out of his grasp, searching through her purse. "Let me give you Brad Quinn's phone number. . . ."

"No rush," he told her. "I'll get the number from you later."

She gave him an incredulous stare. "This is why you came all the way to Boston," she said. "To get your hands on that antique furniture. And now you say there's no rush?"

Simon lowered his voice. "I didn't come to Boston to guarantee a furniture deal. I came to be with you. I came in case you needed me."

I do need you, Simon. He could see Frankie's words from the night before reflected in her wide brown eyes. She was remembering, as clearly as he was, the way she'd clung to him.

"I'm okay now," she told him, her voice just as soft.

"Are you?"

"Yes." She turned abruptly away from him, toward Dominic, suddenly businesslike and brisk. "Am I finished here?"

Dom nodded, flashing Simon a look. "You too, sir. Good luck, sir."

How could she deny that her life hadn't been unconditionally altered by the love they'd shared the night before? How could she pretend that her entire world hadn't been turned upside down and inside out? Simon wanted to grab her and shake some sense into her. Instead, he forced himself to relax, to smile.

Frankie wanted him to disappear. She couldn't

have been more clear about that if she'd told him bluntly to get lost.

But he wasn't going to do that. In fact, he was going to do his best to be very un-lost.

She hadn't been honest when she'd told him she wanted nothing more than a one-night stand. He *had* to believe that. And sooner or later she wasn't going to be able to keep up this facade of disinterest and he was going to find out how she *really* felt.

He had both patience and time.

She didn't stand a chance.

He hoped.

It was the airline flight from hell.

Frankie closed her eyes, but that didn't help. Simon was sitting inches away from her. Even with her eyes closed, she could smell the unforgettable ghostly scent of his cologne. She could hear him unconcernedly turning the pages of the paperback book he'd picked up at the airport. She could sense his presence with every prickling, tingling inch of her body.

The temptation to give in, to turn to him and be enveloped by his familiar, wonderful warmth, was awfully strong. She could still taste his kisses, still feel the thrill of looking into his incredible blue eyes as he took her places she'd never been before.

Hot, erotic places she was likely never again to go—except maybe in her dreams.

"Francine." Simon's voice sounded low and intimate in her ear.

She opened her eyes to find him watching her. He wasn't smiling, and there was a muscle jumping along the side of his jaw. "Do you want anything to drink?"

Whatever she'd thought he was going to ask her, it certainly wasn't that. But she realized that one of the flight attendants was standing in the aisle with the beverage cart, impatiently waiting to take her order.

Frankie shook her head. "No. Thanks. Nothing, please."

She didn't want a drink. She wanted Simon to throw himself down at her feet and tell her he couldn't live without her. She wanted him to beg her to reconsider, to confess his undying love. She wanted him to ask her to marry him, to have his children, to share a lifetime filled with nights of white-hot loving and days of sunshine and laughter.

Simon opened his soda and drank directly from the can. "Are you awake?" he asked after the flight attendant had moved down the aisle.

"Mostly," she admitted.

"About last night—"

"I'd rather not talk about that," Frankie interrupted. She fluffed the small airline pillow and firmly closed her eyes.

"We *do* need to talk," Simon said, his voice low but almost matter-of-fact. "Because, well, frankly, I want more."

Frankie opened her eyes. He was watching her, that sweet, vulnerable look back in his eyes. He smiled almost apologetically. "Last night wasn't enough," he added.

The temptation was nearly unbearable. All she had to do was lean forward, and she'd be in Simon's arms again. But she'd be trading short-term heaven for long-term hell.

"What exactly would be 'enough'?" she asked him, carefully keeping herself distant and cool.

"I don't know," he admitted. At least he was being honest.

"One night was enough for you and Maia Fox," Frankie pointed out. "But with what's-her-name, that waitress you were dating a few months ago . . . ?"

"Amanda."

"That's the one. You spent a whopping month and a half with her," Frankie said. "Perhaps I fall somewhere in between the two?"

"Is that what this is about?" Simon's eyes narrowed.

"No." Frankie wished desperately that he weren't sitting so damned close. "Yes. I don't know. All I know is that sleeping with you last night was a mistake that I'm not going to make again." She leaned toward him, speaking softly, intensely. "We're friends, Si. If we leave last night as a one-night stand—as one wild night of great sex—then we can still be friends. But if we become lovers and turn this into a full-blown affair, then one of us is going to wind up hurt. And then we won't be friends anymore. We'll have awkward, awful uncomfortableness between us. We'll avoid each other, and that'll really suck."

He touched the side of her face. "Francine . . ."

Frankie pulled away. "Simon, *don't.*"

"I can't just shut it off this way!"

His voice was low, but his intensity carried far. People were starting to look in their direction. Frankie took a deep breath, and when she spoke her voice betrayed none of her upset.

"You had no trouble in the past," she told him. "In fact, you're the king when it comes to shutting your feelings down, remember? You can get tired of a woman overnight, and then you're out of there. I'm not going to wait for that to happen—and it's just too bad if you don't like it. I'm getting out now—before I become emotionally involved."

"You're telling me you're *not* emotionally involved?"

"That's right. And I'd like to keep it that way." She lowered her voice to a soft whisper. "Let's leave last night alone. We gave in to our demons, and it was—"

"Fun?" he supplied, his voice rough.

"It was physical, Simon," she told him. "It was *sex.*"

Simon ran his fingers through his hair. His face looked drawn and harsh, his eyes mirroring his pain. He looked tragically handsome and excruciatingly attractive. Frankie had to look out the window.

"It's my reputation coming back to haunt me, isn't it?" he said, true regret in his voice. "You don't want this to go any further because you think I'll dump you in a week or two."

"I don't just think it, Simon." She studied the cotton-puff tops of the clouds. "I know it."

"How long do you want?" he asked, his voice low, imploring.

She glanced at him. "What?"

"A month and a half's not long enough, right? You want longer, right? How long?"

Frankie laughed in disbelief. "You're kidding."

"I'm dead serious."

"You're going to sign your name in blood to some contract or something that promises me you won't walk away before a set amount of time?"

"No, but I'll give you my word."

He was actually serious. He wanted her to set some arbitrary date before which he wouldn't leave her. "That's really stupid, Si. What am I supposed to say? A year? Two? Shoot, I'd feel as if I were signing a lease for a lover. That's not what I want."

He took her hand, lacing their fingers together. His touch was seductive, sensuous. He'd touched her all over with those same fingers last night. Frankie prayed he couldn't feel her accelerated heartbeat.

"What *do* you want?" he asked.

"Forever." The word was out of her mouth before she could stop it. Her first reaction was to squeeze her eyes shut, to deny that she had admitted such foolishness. But instead she found herself gazing up into Simon's crystal-blue eyes, hoping . . .

She found herself wishing she *had* looked away. His pupils shrank to a pinpoint as he stared out the window at the blinding white of the clouds. His gaze became unfocused, almost glazed, and the dancing muscle in the side of his jaw stopped moving. She imagined he looked pale under his tan and his grip loosened on her hand enough for her to slip free.

At her movement, he glanced at her, unable to fully meet her gaze. He tried to smile, but it looked pained, sickly. "Frankie . . ." He laughed, a small gasp of air, and shook his head very slightly. He clearly didn't know what to say.

"Yeah, that's what I thought." Frankie stood up, pushing her way past his knees to the aisle. "I want the man I'm in a relationship with at least to be able to consider the possibility of something permanent. And that's why I'm not going to touch you again, my friend, even with a ten-foot pole. That's why I won't even consider last night as anything more than a one-time event." She opened the overhead compartment and took out her carry-on bag. "So, in that case, what I want is space. A little time and distance, please."

She walked toward the back of the plane to several rows of empty seats.

Simon didn't call her name, didn't follow her.

She hadn't expected that he would.

THIRTEEN

Simon stood on the front porch of the house on Pelican Street and rang the bell for the fifth time that afternoon.

Dammit, he knew Frankie was in there.

They'd been back on the key for nearly a week, and she was doing her best to avoid him. And her best was very, very good.

He stood absolutely still, waiting, listening for any sounds from inside the big old house, but heard nothing. Of course not. She was sitting just as still, waiting for him to leave before she got back to work packing up Alice Winfield's things.

He'd cornered her the day before outside Millie's Market and invited her to dinner. She'd refused. Her brown eyes had been cool, her body language detached, aloof, and her words polite. Her message was clear: She wasn't interested. Yet she'd managed to stall her car four times on the way out of the parking lot.

Simon simply couldn't believe that Frankie felt absolutely nothing for him. He didn't buy it, he refused to accept it.

She was lying to him, and she was lying to herself, and he was going to prove it to her—if he could only get her alone.

He was a master at seduction, and he intended to use his skills shamelessly if he had to. Because once he had her in his arms, once the power of their combined passion took effect, there was no way in hell she could claim that what they shared was casual or insignificant. And then he would convince her that there was a happy medium between all and nothing.

He wasn't quite so confident about his ability to overcome the little problem with "forever." The concept was not one he'd worked with. Ever. The truth was, he hadn't given it very much thought over the past few days. He was focusing on his immediate need to see Frankie again. That was his first priority. He'd worry about the other stuff when the time came.

If only he could find her . . .

What he needed was a private detective.

Simon smiled. He had a private detective. *Frankie* was a private detective. Suddenly the pieces all fell neatly into place and he had a plan.

It would no doubt make her mad, and she'd come in search of him, spitting fire. But he'd make sure that when she found him, he'd be alone.

❖———❖

After checking to make sure Simon wasn't hanging around, Frankie let herself out of Alice Winfield's old house. She'd been going there every day for the past week, boxing up Alice's clothes and dishes and books and seeing they got delivered to various charitable organizations both on the island and on the mainland. The books went to the local nursing home. The clothes to the Salvation Army. The dishes to the church for a future rummage sale.

Alice's photo albums went onto a specially cleared shelf in Frankie's living room.

And Frankie went outside only when the coast was clear and Simon wasn't around.

Every day, two or three or sometimes even four times a day, he would show up at the big old house on Pelican Street and ring the doorbell. She would stay very, very still, like a sailor on a submarine, afraid that the least little noise would give away her location and start a barrage of emotional depth charges.

She wasn't sure how much longer she could last.

It was getting very old, very fast. And the cool distance she struggled to maintain the few times Simon did manage to catch up with her was getting harder and harder to pull off.

He treated her almost the same as he had before they'd spent the night together. He smiled and joked and even teased. Only the content of his words was different. He was relentless in his invitations. He invited her to dinner, to the movies, for a walk along the beach. He wanted to see her again. He needed to talk to her. He asked her out for a cup of coffee, a soda, a glass of water and an Alka-Seltzer. He suggested they start slowly, stand on the corner, and simply breathe air together. He was upbeat and charming and funny. But he couldn't hide the hurt in his eyes. It was always there, lurking underneath his smile, even when he laughed.

That hurt made her feel awful, like some kind of terrible, cold monster. If he only knew how much she missed him . . .

She missed his cheerful smile, his wicked grin. She missed the way he'd drink cup after cup after cup of coffee in the morning until he fully woke up, until his eyes turned from sleepy blue to sharp, neon turquoise. She missed his sarcastic humor and cutting remarks. She missed the way his eyes sparkled like the waters of the Gulf of Mexico, deceptively refreshing and pure. And she missed the soft tenderness of his kisses, sweet kisses that could turn to a blazing inferno of desire in the space of a single heartbeat.

She had to get away from the key soon, or he *would* know.

According to Clay Quinn, her payment and bonus money for finding John Marshall would arrive via bank transfer on Friday. She'd already decided that she was going to make an immediate withdrawal, and take a long-needed vacation. Where? She didn't know yet. Maybe New York City. Maybe New Orleans. Maybe someplace as close as Disney World. It didn't really matter *where* she went—as long as it was far enough away from Simon Hunt.

She pulled her car up in front of her house, idling

for a moment to make sure Simon wasn't in the bushes, waiting to pop out the moment she cut the engine. But there was no sign of him.

She almost wished there were.

Shaking her head in disgust at herself, Frankie climbed wearily out of her car. She hadn't been sleeping well since she'd returned to Sunrise Key. Maybe tonight she'd finally get some rest and she wouldn't feel so worn down, so ready to give in to Simon's persistence.

She saw it before she even reached the porch. It stood out in the deepening twilight—a bright white envelope taped to the inside of her screen door.

The door screeched as she pulled it open and detached the envelope from the screen. The flap hadn't been sealed, and Frankie opened it, pulling out two pieces of paper.

The first was a check for one thousand dollars, from the account of Antiques, Art, and Alligators, Inc., Simon's company, and it was signed with Simon's familiar flourish. On the line marked "For" he'd written the word *Retainer*.

Frankie looked at the other piece of paper. It was blank. She turned it over. There were only two words written on it, again in Simon's big, bold handwriting.

It said, "Find me."

The thousand dollars was indeed a retainer for her services. Simon was hiring her—to find *him*.

Frankie would have laughed at the absurdity of it all if she hadn't felt so much like crying.

All the lights were on inside Simon's sprawling beach house. Frankie pulled up out front and sat gazing at the place. The circular drive was filled with cars and the windows were open, and strains of music—it sounded like Garth Brooks's new CD—spilled out.

Simon was having a party.

It figured he'd plan something like this, that there'd be some reason she wouldn't be able to take his retainer check and tear it into a hundred tiny pieces and throw it into his face the way she wanted. Because as much as she wanted to do that, she wouldn't do it with an audience looking on.

She got out of her car, aware that she was buzzing with anticipation. She was going to see Simon. She was going to gaze into his ocean-blue eyes, see his familiar warm smile.

She'd hand him back his check and tell him nice try.

He'd pull her into his arms, insist on dancing with her.

She'd allow herself *that* much. One dance. She'd let herself relax into his embrace. She'd let herself pretend things were very different between them. It was no more or less than what she used to do when she danced with him at parties.

Frankie didn't bother ringing the doorbell. She just walked inside and headed directly for the kitchen. If Simon wasn't in his kitchen, cooking up some odd hors d'oeuvre, he'd come breezing in soon enough.

She pushed open the door—and caught Leila and Marsh in the middle of an outrageously steamy clinch.

"Oops." Frankie switched swiftly into reverse, trying desperately not to notice whose hands and mouths were where.

But Leila just smiled as she pulled away from her fiancé, not at all flustered. "Oh, good," she said to Frankie, adjusting her clothes and attempting to smooth her blond curls back into place. "You remembered."

Marsh looked embarrassed enough for the both of them. He stood leaning against the kitchen counter, legs and arms crossed, a slightly pained, slightly amused gleam in his normally cool brown eyes. Leila had told her that the seemingly aloof Englishman kept his passionate side neatly hidden from the rest of the world, but Frankie had doubted its very existence—until then.

"Oh, good, I remembered what?"

"My party for Marsh's brother, Jesse. He's decided to stay on the key until the end of the summer. I thought this would be a good way for him to get to know our friends." Leila picked up a knife and began cutting cauliflower into bite-sized chunks. "I told you about it the day you got back from Boston, but you were acting really weird and I wasn't sure you heard a single word I said. I wasn't sure you were going to come."

"Actually," Frankie said, trying to sound sorry, "I can't stay. I just stopped by to drop something off for Simon."

"He's not here." Marsh spoke for the first time. "He called me this afternoon and told me something had come up—he wasn't going to make it to the party."

Frankie narrowed her eyes, trying to curb her sudden sharp disappointment. If Simon wasn't here, where had he gone? *Find me.* "Since when does Simon pass on a party? Especially one at his own house?"

Leila exchanged a look with Marsh. "We were wondering the same thing—and thinking maybe *you* could tell *us* what was going on."

Frankie looked steadily at Marsh. Marsh Devlin was Simon's best friend. There were no secrets between the two men. Or were there? As if he could read her mind, Marsh shook his head very slightly.

"He hasn't told me anything about Boston," Marsh said. "He hasn't said a word." He glanced at Leila and smiled. "We, of course, have done a great deal of speculating. A great, *great* deal. In fact, it's quite become the mystery of the month. You go to Boston, Simon follows in hot pursuit, and when you return, you both go into deep hiding—together? Separately? Who could know? It's all very clandestine and romantic."

"It's driving me crazy," Leila admitted. She scooped the cauliflower into a pretty pink glass bowl and turned to gaze steadily at Frankie. "Are you and Simon . . . ?"

Frankie shook her head. "No. Nothing happened in Boston," she lied.

Leila looked at Marsh. "She's definitely lying. She

gets that little I'm-so-innocent look in her eyes whenever she lies."

Marsh laughed. "Whether she's lying or not, I'd hazard a guess that she was giving you a hint to mind your own business."

Leila gazed at Frankie, her eyes probing, penetrating. Frankie had been avoiding Leila these past few days, as well as Simon. She couldn't hide the truth from her best friend—at least not for long.

And the truth was, despite Frankie's attempt to gain perspective through time and distance, she was still horribly, wretchedly, in love with Leila's brother. The truth was, she had come here tonight, hoping to see Simon, to talk to him, to be near him, to dance with him, and yes, even to let him seduce her again.

Leila's gaze softened. "Are you all right?" she asked quietly.

"I've got to go," Frankie told her. "I'll call you, okay?"

She escaped from the kitchen and out the front door, into the heat of the early evening, wishing there were a breeze to cool her suddenly too hot cheeks.

Find me.

If she were Simon, where would she be?

Back in her car, Frankie cruised past the Pelican Street house, past the ice cream parlor, past the Rustler's Hideout, past Millie's Market, but there was no sign of Simon's sports car. She wasn't sure if she felt disappointment or relief.

She pulled into her own driveway at a little past

eight-thirty and went into her office to think. She sat down at her desk and put her head in her hands.

Find me.

Simon had made this slightly more challenging than she at first had thought. But there was no way he would make it *too* difficult for her to find him. He *wanted* her to find him, that much she had to believe.

He wanted her to find him as much as she did. And she did.

It was clear that the only person she'd fooled over the past week was herself.

Frankie took both Simon's check and the note from her pocket and spread them out in front of her on her desk. *Find me.* He'd written the words in black ink, probably with one of those silver pens that he kept in his appointment book. She could picture him holding the slender, elegant pen with his long, equally elegant fingers. She could picture those same fingers lightly trailing their way down her body followed by the softness of his mouth. . . .

She forced her mind to switch gears and picked up the note. The paper was thick. It was an expensive, linen-content heavyweight bond suitable for a formal letter from someone with lots of numbers and esquires after their name. She'd seen this kind of paper recently. But where?

Frankie turned on her desk lamp, holding the paper up to the bulb. It was an elegant off-white color, the same as . . .

She dug in her purse for her wallet and pulled out the slip of paper she'd stuck in with her dollar bills, the piece of paper upon which Clay Quinn had written his brother's phone number.

Yes. It was a direct match. And she knew for a fact that Clay had gotten that fancy paper from the Seaholm Resort.

Frankie reached for the phone book and quickly looked up the main number for the resort. She picked up her phone and dialed the number.

"Seaholm Resort."

"Hi," Frankie said. "Can you tell me if Simon Hunt is registered there?"

"One moment, please."

Frankie tapped her fingers on her desk. He *had* to be there. He *had* to be.

"Yes, he is. Shall I connect you to his room?"

"No! I mean, thank you, no." Frankie hung up the phone. Okay. She found him.

Now what?

She had two options. Go there and inevitably end up in his bed. Or *not* go there, stay home, and cry herself to sleep because the man that she'd been unlucky enough to fall in love with wasn't perfect.

Frankie knew she would be miserable with Simon, but she was miserable without him.

At least if she was with him, she'd be guaranteed a few weeks or even months of happiness. True, it would be pseudo-happiness, but that was better than what she was doing to herself right now, wasn't it?

Find me.

She wanted to. She wanted to find him.

Frankie rested her forehead in the palms of her

hands, knowing what she had known even on the airplane home from Boston.

She was going to give in. She was going to surrender—she was going to play this game by Simon's rules. But before she did that, she was going to give Simon a chance to quit while he was ahead. She was going to give him a chance to walk away.

It didn't seem too unreasonable. She'd sit down with Simon, her lifelong friend, and simply tell him the truth. She'd tell him that somehow, at some point during the past nearly twenty years, she'd gone and foolishly fallen in love with him. She wouldn't wait for him to see her feelings in her eyes, in the way she held him, touched him, loved him. It would be out in the open, on the table, there for him to deal with—or to walk away from.

She squeezed her eyes shut. Lord, she couldn't imagine actually saying those words. *I'm in love with you. . . .*

But wait a minute. Frankie opened her eyes. Maybe she didn't have to actually use words. Maybe she could get the message across in another, far less painful way.

She stood up and went upstairs to search the far reaches of her bedroom closet.

FOURTEEN

Simon checked his watch for the four thousandth time since sundown.

It was four minutes after nine o'clock.

He'd told himself several hours before that if Frankie didn't show up by nine, she wasn't going to show up at all.

Yet here it was, after nine. He'd give her another ten minutes. . . .

But then what?

He sat in the dark, out on the screened-in balcony of his room at the Seaholm Resort, listening to the sound of the ocean murmuring below, feeling his frustration build.

He kept coming back to the same damned question: How could Frankie just ignore what they'd had together? How could she just walk away from the magic they'd found? How could she deny the fact that what they'd shared had been soul-shattering, heart-wrenching, mind-blowing true love? How could she stand there and say "I need some distance," instead of "I love you"? How could she . . .

Simon gazed up at the stars, his eyes out of focus.

How could *he*? Because, when it came right down to it, *he* was doing some heavy-duty denial of his own. He was saying the wrong words too. He was saying "I want you" and "I need you" when he *should* have been saying "I love you." And he did. He loved Frankie with a strength that rocked him to his very soul. He loved her absolutely, purely, completely. Endlessly.

And it was about time he admitted that to himself.

She wasn't going to come here tonight. So now what was he going to do?

Give her that forever she was looking for. Ask her to marry him.

The thought was no longer as frightening as it had been a week earlier. It still made him feel rather short of breath, but it no longer stopped his heart.

The thought of losing Frankie, of never holding her in his arms again, of seeing her beautiful smile only from a safe, sterile distance . . . *that* made Simon's heart stop.

He stood up, slightly light-headed, determined to find Frankie and fall down on his knees in front of her if he had to.

He'd start with "I love you," and pray that that worked. If it didn't, he was going to have to do it. He was going to have to ask her to marry him. Because he could not and would not spend another day like this past one.

He checked the pockets of his pants for his car keys as he headed out into the living room of his hotel suite and—

Frankie.

Simon stopped short, his heart in his throat.

She was standing just inside the door, wearing . . . Oh, my God, she was wearing it. She'd sworn she never, ever would, but she was wearing it. The black dress. The one Simon had found in her closet, the one that had appeared in his dreams so many times since then.

It looked even better on her than he'd imagined. It had narrow straps that accentuated her smooth bare shoulders. It clung snugly to her breasts, flaring out into a very short skirt. She was actually wearing stockings on her gorgeous legs. They were sheer and black and ended in a pair of black high heels.

Frankie moistened her lips nervously. "In case you were wondering, I got the shoes for the occasion."

Simon's mouth was dry too, but somehow he managed to ask, "And what exactly *is* the occasion?"

"My surrender," she said.

Yes. Thank God. Simon couldn't keep his sudden rush of relief and triumph from showing in his eyes, in his smile, in his quickly drawn-in breath.

"Before you get too excited," she warned him, "you might want to hear my terms."

He didn't care. Whatever her terms were, he'd take 'em. My God, she was wearing *the dress.* Two weeks ago she'd implied she'd wear that dress only for someone who was extraordinary, someone special, someone whom perhaps she loved. . . . The thought made him giddy and he laughed. "Terms," he repeated. "You mean, like the release of prisoners of war?"

She smiled at his joke, but her eyes still looked sad.

"You look like someone died," he said softly, moving toward her. "This isn't *really* that awful, is it, Francine?"

"First things first." She obviously wasn't going to answer his question. She held out his retainer check as if it would help ward him off. "I can't take this."

Simon crossed his arms. "No, you earned it. I hired you to find me, and you did."

"I *wanted* to find you."

"I'm glad." Simon's heart was singing. In his mind he was doing a victory dance around the room, whooping and jumping and hollering.

"It suddenly seemed so silly," she explained. "I was pretending something very real didn't exist and—" She held out the check again. "Here. Take this back, will you?"

Simon took the check and held on to Frankie's hand, tugging her closer to him. "Have you had dinner?" he asked. "Do you want to go downstairs—to the restaurant? Or we could order room service . . . ?"

She turned away from him slightly, and he realized that her dress left nearly her entire back bare. The dress was held together by a series of strips of fabric, crossing and crisscrossing and tying near her waist. He wanted to dance with her, to hold her close, to feel all that smooth skin beneath his fingers.

"I'm not particularly hungry," she said. "Although if you are, you could order something . . ."

"What *I* want has nothing to do with food," Simon told her with a smile. "But it seems a shame to take off your dress after waiting so long for you to put it *on*." He pulled her toward the balcony. "Come on. I have a bottle of wine on ice. Why don't we have a glass while we negotiate these terms of yours?"

Frankie was aware of the warmth of Simon's hand, aware of the heat in his eyes. He didn't seem a bit fazed by the silent message her dress sent forth. "They're nonnegotiable," she told him.

Out on the balcony, Simon had several candles burning, and their flames twitched and jumped, casting a flickering, romantic light filled with shadows and mystery.

He turned to look at her as he skillfully opened the bottle of wine. He was at home in the softness of the candlelight, with a wine bottle in his hand and a small smile playing about the corners of his lips. She was in his territory now, Frankie realized. This was the scene of a well-thought-out seduction, and he was a master at the game.

She sat down, aware that his eyes followed the movement of her legs as she crossed them.

She murmured her thanks as he handed her a glass of wine and sat down across from her, sideways on the long seat of a chaise longue.

He took a sip of his wine as he gazed at her, his

elbows resting on his knees, his eyes intense, his attention completely hers.

Frankie cleared her throat. "You remember asking me how long I wanted?"

He nodded.

"Well, I've thought about it, and maybe it's not as stupid as it first seemed. It occurred to me that maybe you'd actually be able to handle a longer-term relationship if you knew for certain that you had an out—if there was a predetermined date that it would end. Do you remember the winter I worked pumping septic tanks, replacing Andy Kraft while he was in Alabama, taking care of his daughter's kids while she was in the hospital? It was an awful job, despite the fact that it paid well. But I got through it, because I knew I wasn't going to be pumping septic tanks for the rest of my life. I knew that Andy would be back on April twenty-ninth, and I'd be free."

Simon took another sip of wine, unable to hide his smile. "Are you actually comparing yourself to a septic tank that needs pumping?"

"I'd be willing to bet that I smell better, but yes, I am."

He shook his head in disbelief. "You are so *not* a septic tank—symbolically or otherwise."

"Four months," Frankie said. "I've thought hard about it, and four months seems fair, don't you think?"

"Francine, this is—"

"This is the way I want to do it, Simon. Four months puts us at the end of August. At that time I'll take a two-week off-island vacation. When I get back, you'll be gone for another two weeks. You can plan whatever you want—a vacation, a buying trip, whatever. You just have to promise to disappear for at least two weeks, okay?"

Simon gazed at Frankie's face in the candlelight. She was dead serious. And she fully expected him to agree. It was weird, setting an end date to a relationship.

He'd been ready to ask her to marry him.

Well, perhaps not exactly *ready*. More like prepared as best as possible, ready in case he had to.

Four months. It seemed so arbitrary. How could he possibly know now what he'd feel in four months?

Frankie was looking away from him, down at her shoes, her confidence fading at his extended silence. When she glanced up at him, her eyes were apologetic. "I know this is crazy," she said. "Even if you agree to this, there's no way I can hold you to it. But I just thought—"

"It's fine," Simon interrupted. He would have said anything to remove that anxious look from her face.

Strains of music drifted up, probably from someone else's room. Simon stood up, holding his hand out to Frankie. "Dance with me."

Heart in her throat, Frankie went into his waiting arms. This was no fantasy. Simon was hers—at least for the next four months.

She had to stop thinking that way. Four months was a very long time. She could very well be sick of him at the end of four months.

She closed her eyes at the sensation of his hands on her back, his fingers caressing her daringly exposed skin. His touch felt sinfully good and Frankie felt redeemed. She might have given in, but already it was worth it.

His arms tightened around her, pulling her closer, and he leaned down to brush his smooth-shaven cheek against hers as he whispered in her ear, "I'm not sure you're going to want to hear this, but I think we're dancing to the music from a toilet paper commercial playing on someone's television set."

Frankie had to laugh. And she knew for a solid fact that after four months, four years, or even four decades, she would *never* be sick of Simon Hunt.

"Years from now we'll meet in a bar in Casablanca," she said, smiling up into his eyes, "and you'll say, 'Play it, Sam. Play that toilet paper commercial. . . .'"

"From now on Angel Soft will have a special place in my heart," Simon teased.

For the next four months, at least . . . Frankie shook her head. She *had* to stop thinking that way. She put her arms around his neck. "Kiss me, Si."

"With pleasure," he murmured, his lips brushing hers, first lightly, then harder but still so sweetly.

Frankie angled her head, deepening the kiss, attempting to exorcise all her pessimistic thoughts through the delicious taste of his mouth, through the erotic sensation of his tongue against hers.

He kissed her slowly, languorously, taking his sweet time to thoroughly possess her mouth, and she felt herself melting as time dragged way out and slowed way down.

At this rate, four months could last a lifetime.

His fingers found the bow that held her dress on, and the zipper right below it. He deftly unfastened both, and Frankie felt her dress fall off her, pooling in a puddle of silk at her feet.

Hers was a vulnerable position to be in. While Simon was still fully dressed, she was half naked. She wore only her shoes and thigh-high stockings, and the black lace panties Leila had purchased when she'd bought this dress. But the breeze coming in from the gulf was warm, and the look in Simon's eyes was positively hot. She didn't feel at all exposed.

"I have this fantasy," he whispered, his hands skimming the length of her body, "that involves us actually making love in a bed."

"Slowly?" Frankie felt herself tremble as his mouth replaced his hands on her breasts.

"Incredibly slowly," he murmured, hooking his fingers in her panties and dragging them down her legs.

"I may die. Because, see, I like it fast. . . ." She reached for his belt buckle, but he stopped her hands.

"Nuh-uh. Not this time. First we get over to the bed. I'm not taking any chances here." He picked up a candle and led her slowly, step by step, across the hotel suite and into the bedroom.

It was perfect. He was standing, looking at her, so much desire and need on his face. His tie was askew, his shirt rumpled, and his blond hair fell across his forehead into his eyes. But it didn't matter what he was wearing or not wearing. It didn't matter if they made love on this enormous bed or swinging from the chandeliers. What mattered was his quicksilver smile, the gleam of excitement and amusement sparkling in his eyes, the fact that he could find something to laugh about no matter the situation.

Frankie knew that in all of her fantasies, romantic or otherwise, there had always been one constant—Simon.

He set the candle down on a table next to the bed and crossed toward her. He kissed her, slowly again, deliberately.

Frankie stepped out of her shoes and pulled him back with her, down onto the bed.

He kissed her again, filling her, surrounding her, covering her with his familiar scent, his warmth, his need.

His love.

It was easy to pretend that he loved her totally and completely as he touched and caressed—worshiped—every inch of her body with his hands and his mouth. He took his sweet time, moving excruciatingly slowly, pulling away when she tried to unbutton his shirt or unfasten his belt.

It took forever, a long, sensuous, exquisite forever, but Frankie finally got his shirt off. Near delirious with the sensation, she ran her hands across the smooth muscles of his back and pressed her bare breasts against his chest.

He groaned as he covered her face with kisses, and

together they rid him of his pants and shorts. It took him several seconds to cover himself and protect them both, and then he was back beside her.

He pulled her on top of him, entwining their legs and arms, and she closed her eyes, delighting in the sensation of flesh against flesh, soft against hard. He rolled her back around so that she was once more beneath him. She could feel the hard length of his arousal pressed against her belly, and she marveled at his restraint.

She looked up to find his eyes open, a smile on his beautifully shaped lips as he watched her.

"What other fantasies do you have?" she asked breathlessly. "Because we seem to be handling this making - love - in - bed - and - taking - it - really - slowly fantasy pretty damn well."

His smile widened. "I've got a real good one that involves you and me and the hotel elevator."

"I've got a major thing for the butcher-block counter in your kitchen," Frankie admitted.

"Just the butcher block?" Simon asked, his eyes dancing. "Or do I play a part in it too?"

"You've got the starring role," she told him. She reached up to touch the side of his face with her hand and felt her heart soften as she gazed into the amazing blue eyes of this man who had been her friend for so many years, this man who was now her lover. "It's always been you, Si."

She could see wonder in his eyes, wonder and a joy she'd never seen before. "Say it," he breathed. "I want to hear you say it."

He could read her mind. Frankie knew he could, knew exactly what he wanted to hear. And she knew that by giving him that, she would be giving him everything. There'd be nothing left to hide behind, nothing left to pretend.

"I knew it was what you were telling me when you wore that dress," he whispered, "but I want to hear the words. Please, Francine . . ."

Frankie moistened her lips. "I love you."

She could have sworn she saw tears appear in Simon's eyes. But then he pulled her close, capturing her mouth in the sweetest of kisses as he slowly and completely filled her.

He moved excruciatingly slowly, and when she would have quickened the pace, he stopped her. Her blood was pounding crazily through her veins as each stroke seemed to take a century to complete.

"Simon—" She opened her eyes to find him watching her again. His face was a picture of intensity, his hair damp and curling with perspiration. "Please . . ."

"Don't fight it, Frankie," he murmured. "Savor it, go with it. . . . The same way you let yourself love me, let me love you."

Frankie's dark eyes flashed as she met Simon's steady gaze, but he knew that she decided not to question him as she closed her eyes and lifted her lips for a kiss.

She opened her mouth to him, allowing him to invade her completely, and he felt his own control start to slip. But then he felt her sigh at his caress, felt her begin to relax, moving with him at the pace he set, giving in to his control.

She trusted him. Simon felt a flash of joy nearly as intense as the pleasure he was getting from making love to her.

She trusted him and loved him enough to risk *everything*—her pride, her self-respect, her heart. He knew Frankie well enough to know that these were not things she'd give up easily.

She moaned a long-drawn-out sigh of pleasure at each of his movements, and he felt his body respond eagerly to the knowledge that she was close to her release.

"Simon . . ." He felt the beginning of her climax as she breathed his name, felt her body clench and tighten around him as she was pushed over the edge. It was all he'd been waiting for. He felt his own release in slow motion, somersaulting through him, bursting through his veins, exploding in his brain.

And it was then, right there and then, in the aftermath of the explosion, even before Simon could remember something so simple as his name, that he knew.

He didn't *need* to marry Frankie. He didn't *have* to marry Frankie. He *wanted* to marry her.

As she clung to him, still rocked by the intensity of their lovemaking, Simon realized that his most perfect fantasy of all was well within his reach.

A wife—a lover and friend—to laugh with by day and burn with at night. Children—daughters and sons. A sense of peace and belonging he'd never had before . . .

"Si, would you mind if we extend our little agreement for another four months?" Frankie's voice sounded sleepy in his ear. "Because I want to spend at *least* that long making love to you just like this—nice and slow."

Simon had to laugh as he rolled over, pulling her into his arms. "I wouldn't dream of doing that to you," he said. "It'd be torture. You've made it more than clear that you like making love only hard and fast."

Frankie leaned her head against his shoulder, using one hand to outline the muscles on his chest. "That's just like you to prove your point," she said lightly, "and then make sure you really rub it in."

"I love you."

Frankie froze, her palm resting over Simon's heart. She lifted her head and met his warm blue gaze.

"I do," he added.

She shook her head. "Simon, don't mess things up that way. Just because *I* said it doesn't mean you have to—"

"Marry me, Frankie."

It took several seconds for her heart to start beating again, several more before she could speak. Even then, her voice shook. "Bad joke, Hunt."

"It's not—"

"Don't." She pulled away from him. "Please. Don't ruin this by saying something I know you couldn't possibly mean."

"But I *do* mean it. Francine, I've never been more serious in my entire—"

"Shhh." She covered his mouth with her hand. "We made our agreement. Four months. If you still feel the same way in four months, well, we'll talk. But I'm not going to spend the next four months with you feeling nervous and trapped by something you said without thinking it through. I'm going to pretend you never said that. I never heard those words."

"But, Francine—"

"Simon, *please*. I *know* you."

There were tears in her eyes, threatening to overflow, and Simon backed down. "All right. You win."

He was rewarded by a kiss and a sweetly sad smile.

"I'm so tired," Frankie murmured. "Mind if I close my eyes?"

He pushed her hair back from her face. "Not if you don't mind if I wake you up later."

She smiled sleepily. "For more dancing to the music from toilet paper commercials? Definitely."

She sighed and shifted into a more comfortable position, her movement taking her out of his arms and turning her away from him. She was already asleep, Simon realized, her breathing slow and steady.

Even in her sleep she was taking care not to cling to him. Even in her sleep she was careful to give him space, to keep her distance.

She said she knew him. But she didn't. She didn't believe him when he spoke directly from his heart.

Of course, she hadn't had the opportunity to read

his diaries. Of course, he hadn't kept diaries, so that put them both at a disadvantage.

But he *did* love her. And he wanted to marry her. Not in four months. Now. He wanted to know today that she was his not just for the next four months, but until the end of time. He wanted that with a conviction that crushed all of his fear, that left him without a single lingering doubt.

But how to make Frankie believe him?

FIFTEEN

Simon quietly slipped out of bed and gathered his clothes from the floor. He went into the hotel suite's living room, closing the bedroom door gently behind him.

He quickly got dressed, then picked up the telephone and dialed the resort's front desk.

"Front desk. How can I help you?"

Simon blinked, recognizing the smoky voice on the other end, made raspy from a two-pack-a-day nicotine habit. "Pres?" he asked the resort owner. "What the hell are *you* doing working the front desk?"

"Simon Hunt." Preston Seaholm recognized Simon's voice as well. If he was at all curious as to why Simon was staying in one of his most expensive rooms when he had a perfectly good house on Sunrise Key, he didn't say a word. "My night concierge called to say he'd be late, and my evening concierge couldn't stay—hot date, I think. I actually like to fill in every now and then—keeps my finger on the pulse of the place. Now, if I could only find a day guy who's as dependable—"

Simon sat up. "Are you looking? Because I recently stayed at the Parker House in Boston, and in my book, there's a concierge up there who gets a twenty on a scale from one to ten. His name's Dominic Defeo, and he's worth top dollar. More. And whatever you pay him, you'll get twice your money's worth. Call him—tell him you're a friend of mine."

Simon could hear Preston writing the name down. "I will. Thanks for the tip. God, if this works out, I'll owe you one. Oh . . . here's Manuel now." There was a pause, then Simon heard Pres say, "No, no—I've got this one, thanks. It's a friend of mine." Pres returned his attention to Simon. "So like I said at the start of this call, how can I help you?"

"I need a notebook," Simon said.

"Hmm. I know I have some legal pads in my office."

"It's got to be spiral bound."

"Like something a kid would use for school?"

"Exactly."

"I've seen them at the convenience store downtown," Pres said. "It's open for another . . . twenty minutes."

"Any chance I can get someone to run out and pick one up for me? I can't leave to get it myself."

"It's that important?"

"Yeah."

"Then it's not a problem. Now that Manny's here, I can do it myself."

"*You* . . . ?"

"See you in a few."

"Don't you even want to know what I need the notebook for?"

Preston laughed. "Absolutely. But right now I'm your host. It would be rude to ask. But you better believe the day you check out of here, I'm going to show up at your office as your *friend*, and then you're going to tell me what this is all about. And it better be good."

"Oh, it is," Simon said with a slow smile. "It's incredibly good."

Frankie woke up as Simon slipped into bed beside her and kissed her.

Sunlight was streaming in beneath the heavy curtains and there was the most wonderful fragrant aroma wafting through the air from the other room.

Simon's kisses tasted like mocha-flavored coffee and croissants. How early had he gotten up and called room service?

"What time is it?" she asked.

He drew her into his arms and kissed her again. "Almost seven. Time for breakfast."

"Seven?" Frankie pulled back from the hypnotizing warmth of his body and the exquisite sensation of their legs tangled together, skin against skin. She could feel his arousal against her, see a reflection of his desire in his eyes. "You're not a morning person. Since when do *you* get up before seven?"

"I didn't exactly *get* up," he said cryptically.

"Then who ordered the room service?"

He just smiled and kissed her again. This time he pushed her away from him when she would have deepened their kiss. "Just go have breakfast."

Frankie was very confused. "You want me to get out of bed . . . now?" He was clearly as hot for her as she was for him, yet he wanted her to . . . have breakfast.

He gave her another gentle push. "Go."

There was a gorgeous silk robe lying at the end of the bed, and Simon reached for it, handing it to her.

She had to laugh. "Simon . . . can't we have breakfast *later*? I want to stay in bed. And I couldn't miss noticing that you—"

"I'll be here when you're done."

Now she was really stumped. "You're not having breakfast?"

"I had mine already." He smiled at her. "Go. Humor me."

Simon settled himself back into the bed as Frankie gazed at him, eyes narrowed. He looked tired, as if he'd been up all night. "What's going on?"

He just smiled.

Frankie pulled on the bathrobe, the silk smooth against her skin, and tied the belt. Giving him one last, long look, she went out the bedroom door and into the living room.

The table on the screened-in balcony was covered

with a linen cloth and set with a sumptuous breakfast feast. There was fresh fruit of all kinds, an elegant thermos of coffee, a basket of freshly baked breads and pastries—including croissants, her favorite. There was juice and jam and butter and honey. And right in the middle of the plate that he had set for her was a note-book. A spiral-bound notebook.

It looked exactly like the inexpensive notebooks she'd used as makeshift diaries since she'd been old enough to write.

Curious, she opened the cover to the front page.

Her name was on it, as well as today's date. But it had another date too. It had an end date listed as nearly a year from now.

And the handwriting wasn't hers. It was Simon's.

What was going on?

She sat down in the chair and, pouring herself a cup of that fragrant coffee, she turned the page.

April 28th, it said at the top. That was today.

"Simon arranged for the most incredible breakfast this morning," she read. "It was waiting for me when I woke up. After breakfast we made love all morning long, and he told me again that he loves me. I'm start-ing to believe him. . . ."

What the hell . . . ?

Had Simon written diary entries for events that hadn't even happened?

She leafed through the notebook, and indeed, it was entirely filled, from front to back, with his bold handwriting. This was too bizarre. He'd written this as if he were *her*, recounting actual events.

She turned back to the first page. *He told me again that he loves me. I'm starting to believe him. . . .*

She quickly turned to the next page.

April 30th. Simon helped me move the last of Alice Winfield's things from her house on Pelican Street. He knew how difficult it would be for me to see the house standing empty, with that forlorn-looking For Sale sign out front. We walked through it together, and he kissed me in every room.

I told him how I'd always dreamed about living in that big old house, how as a kid I'd imagined Gram and me moving in with Alice and staying up late playing gin rummy and Yahtzee every night. As we stood in the parlor, looking out the windows at the view of the ocean, Simon took my hand and asked me to marry him."

Frankie's heart was in her throat.

Before I could say a word, he told me to give him a chance—to hear him out. He told me that he loved me—that he's never loved anyone in his life the way that he loves me. He told me that he's spent his whole life running from that kind of love, afraid that he would end up trapped. He told me that the love he feels for me doesn't trap him—it sets him free. . . .

Frankie's eyes blurred with tears, and she blinked them back, wanting to read more, *needing* to read more of the words he'd obviously stayed up all night to write.

> He said he wants to know I'm always going to be there, every single day, for the rest of his life. He said that I was right when I told him that someday he'd meet a woman that he simply couldn't live without, a woman who was his soul mate, a woman to whom he'd promise to be faithful and true—a woman to whom he'd never break those promises.
>
> He said he must be the biggest fool on the key, because he met that woman a lifetime ago, and it took him twenty years to figure out that it was me he wanted. But now that he's finally got his act together, he said he couldn't wait for four months to tell me all of this.
>
> He wants forever, and he wants it to start today.
>
> Before I could answer, he kissed me, and I could feel him shaking. He was so frightened that I wouldn't believe him—I thought that he might even cry.
>
> He asked me again to marry him, and then he asked me to buy this house with him—to make it ours, to live in happily ever after.
>
> There was plenty of room for both of our offices, he told me, as if I'd need further convincing. And lots of bedrooms in case we

wanted to have kids. "Do you want to have kids?" he asked. "Because if you want, I would truly love to have kids—with you."

I answered him with a kiss.

"I love you," he said, and I knew it was true.

Wiping tears from her face, Frankie turned the page, reading quickly through the months of May and June, unable to keep from laughing as she took in Simon's account of their late spring wedding on the beach, the bride in a white Speedo bathing suit. Each entry ended the same way, with Simon declaring his love, and Frankie knowing that it was true.

July sped by just as quickly, with the two of them settling into the house on Pelican Street. Both of their businesses thrived. Frankie frequently accompanied Simon on his buying trips, and he continued to act as her Dr. Watson when she took on new private investigations.

And then came August.

August 29th. Simon went to Orlando this morning and didn't get back until late tonight. I couldn't help but remember that deal we made back in April—the one that said we'd split come the end of August. I was still awake when Simon came home, and I reminded him of that, and asked him, now that we've been married nearly two months, if he had any regrets.

He told me the only thing he regrets is that he didn't marry me ten years ago. He told me that as much as he loved me in April, he loves me even more now. He told me never to doubt that, ever.

I believed him. And then I told him the news I knew for certain just this morning. I'm pregnant. We're going to have a child.

Simon's response amazed me. He wept. And then he laughed. And then he kissed me. He broke out a bottle of his special nonalcoholic champagne, and we drank it and danced on the back porch until the early hours of the morning, both so incredibly happy. . . .

Frankie closed the notebook, unable to read any more, not needing to read any more.

He loved her. He truly wanted to marry her.

Simon was exhausted, but there was no way on earth he was going to fall asleep.

He could hear Frankie from where she was sitting, out on the balcony. He heard her pour herself a cup of coffee, he heard the pages of the notebook turning as she read his words.

Please God, he prayed. Let this work.

Every now and then he heard her laugh. Laughter was a good sign, wasn't it?

And then he heard the sound of the chair scraping back as she stood up, and he knew this was it. The moment of truth. Literally. Simon could feel his heart pounding.

And then Frankie stood in the doorway.

"I can't believe you did that," she said. "Were you up all night?"

He nodded. "Yeah."

She came into the room, moving closer, and he saw that her eyes were wet. "You really love me."

He laughed with frustration. "God, if you still have to ask, then I better get up and go write some more."

"I wasn't asking," Frankie said. "I was . . . re-marking. With amazement."

"Marry me, Frankie."

She caught her breath in what was half sob, half laughter. "You're not supposed to ask me until the day after tomorrow."

"I don't want to wait that long."

Frankie's tears threatened to overflow, magnifying the love he could see in her eyes. "I don't want to either."

"Marry me," Simon whispered again.

She fell into his arms and answered him with a kiss.

"I love you," he told her.

And she believed him.

THE EDITORS' CORNER

What better way to celebrate the holidays than with four sensual and exciting new LOVESWEPTs. Whether they're searching for treasure or battling bad guys, our heroes are sure to deliver thrills, laughs, and passion as they do whatever they must to win the hearts of our heroines. So curl up in your favorite chair with a blanket and a cup of hot cocoa and enjoy!

Starting off our fabulous lineup is Marcia Evanick with **TANGLED UP IN BLUE**, LOVESWEPT #818. He's expecting a gray-haired housesitter who plays bingo when she isn't baking cookies or dusting, but when Matt Stone returns unannounced, he discovers instead a golden-haired nymph splashing naked in his pool! Beulah Crawford, nicknamed Blue, is the picture of sweet chaos, a delightful scamp who revels in living for the moment. Now all Matt has to do is make her believe that family isn't just an impossible dream. Hailed by *Romantic Times* for "delighting readers with her marvelous blend of love and laughter," Marcia Evanick won't let readers down in this funny tale of cat and mouse romance.

Watch out, villains! Cynthia Powell has found a **HERO FOR HIRE**, LOVESWEPT #819. Cade Jackson has a face too hard to be handsome, Martinique Duval decides, and a smile just lethal enough to make a good girl want to be bad! Tracking his quarry has led the tough bounty hunter straight to this wildfire angel, but keeping her safe means risking a heart he didn't know he had. Can her innocence give a reluctant hero with a scarred soul a reason to stop running forever? Rising star Cynthia Powell proves once again that every man is susceptible to the call of true love.

Talented newcomer Eve Gaddy believes that two people in love can never be **TOO CLOSE FOR COMFORT**, LOVESWEPT #820. Jack Corelli vows to keep Marissa Fairfax alive to testify, but guarding the cool trauma surgeon means long, hot hours in close quarters with a woman who challenges him to break all of his rules! She barely trembles when held at gunpoint, but Jack's slow, sizzling attack on her mouth makes her shiver and burn. Together, this wounded hero and the lady he'd die to protect must learn to silence ghosts and survive a desperate betrayal. Eve Gaddy takes readers on a heart-palpitating ride as she weaves a tale you won't soon forget!

When you're gambling with love, everything is **UP FOR GRABS**, LOVESWEPT #821, by Kristen Robinette. Jesse McCain steps onto her land without asking, a bold buccaneer who knows the stormy-eyed lady won't deny him a chance to dig up her property—and her past! Targeted by a grin full of promises, Lauren Adams feels her resistance melt, but the brash archeologist isn't telling her all he knows. Still, she isn't one to back down from a challenge, so she follows Jesse down an unknown path and ends up losing her heart to a road warrior with a secret. In a debut that readers are sure to enjoy, Kristen delivers a top-notch romance full of tenderness and passion.

Happy reading!

With warmest wishes,

Beth de Guzman

Shauna Summers

Beth de Guzman   Shauna Summers

Senior Editor   Editor

P.S. Watch for these Bantam women's fiction titles coming in January: From Sandra Brown, the author of twenty-nine *New York Times* bestselling titles, comes **HAWK O'TOOLE'S HOSTAGE**, a riveting contemporary romance in which a woman is held hostage by a desperate man . . . and a desperate desire. Now available in paperback, **THE UGLY DUCKLING** is a thrilling novel of contemporary suspense by *New York Times* bestselling author Iris Johansen. From Susan Johnson, mistress of erotic romance, comes **WICKED,** a spectacular romance of suspense and seduction. And finally, **HEART OF THE FALCON** by Suzanne Robinson captures the passion of Egypt as a defiant beauty fights to regain her birthright. Don't miss the previews of these exceptional novels in next month's LOVESWEPTs. And immediately following this page, sneak a peek at the Bantam women's fiction titles on sale *now*!

For current information on Bantam's women's fiction, visit our new web site, *Isn't It Romantic*, at the following address: **http://www.bdd.com/romance**

Don't miss these extraordinary books
by your favorite Bantam authors

On sale in November:

AFTER CAROLINE
by Kay Hooper

BREAKFAST IN BED
by Sandra Brown

DON'T TALK TO STRANGERS
by Bethany Campbell

LORD SAVAGE
by Patricia Coughlin

LOVE'S A STAGE
by Sharon and Tom Curtis

from

Kay Hooper

Her sensuous and evocative voice has made her a
nationally bestselling author, and now she weaves a
haunting new tale of contemporary suspense, a
gripping emotional tapestry of two women bound
together in the desperation of one fatal moment—
and the urgent need to uncover the truth.

AFTER CAROLINE

Joanna Flynn was lucky to be alive. Twice in a matter
of minutes she almost died on a patch of oil-slicked
highway. But when the doctors told her that she
would suffer no lasting effects, they were wrong. For
that night the dreams began. . . .

They were of a house perched high above the sea,
of a ticking clock, and the lingering scent of roses. Yet
night after night Joanna awoke with a sense of panic.
Terror lingered throughout her days, urging her to do
something—but what? Then two strangers on the
street called her Caroline, and Joanna knew she had
to find an explanation for what was happening, or
she'd lose her mind.

What she finally uncovered was an obituary for a
woman named Caroline McKenna—a woman who
looked enough like her to be her twin, a woman who
was killed in a car accident on the same day Joanna
should have perished. Now her torturous nightmares
and a tenuous connection have brought Joanna three
thousand miles across country to the town where
Caroline lived—and died. Almost everyone has stories

to tell about Cliffside's leading lady, and yet no one seems to have known her. Was she the shy wife or the seductress of men? The devoted mother or the selfish beauty?

Too soon Joanna realizes that it's not her sanity at stake, but her life. For unraveling the mystery of Caroline means uncovering the secrets in this picturesque town, secrets someone may have killed to hide. And that someone appears all too willing to kill again.

AVAILABLE IN HARDCOVER

Sandra Brown

Her novels are sensual and moving, compelling and richly satisfying. Now the *New York Times* bestselling author of *Heaven's Price* captures the wrenching dilemma of a woman tempted by an unexpected—and forbidden—love. . . .

BREAKFAST IN BED

Hurt one too many times in the past, Sloan Fairchild is convinced that she will never be able to trust her heart to a man again. Instead, she pours all her energy into making a success of her elegant San Francisco bed-and-breakfast inn. But when her best friend asks her to house her fiancé for a month, Sloan opens the doors of Fairchild House to Carter Madison . . . and meets a man who turns her world—and her concept of herself—upside down.

Carter, a bestselling author, is looking for a little peace and quiet so he can finish his latest novel before his wedding. The last thing he expects is to find himself instantly attracted to his hostess—or her to him. As the days pass, Sloan tries to ignore the feelings this handsome, disturbingly perceptive man stirs in her . . . tries to stop herself from dreaming dreams that can never be. But as Carter reveals his overwhelming desire for her, Sloan is left to struggle against her own deepest longing: to know just once how it feels to be truly cherished.

Caught between love and loyalty to her best friend, Sloan must search her soul and make a choice: to love for the moment, walk away forever, or fight to have it all.

AVAILABLE IN PAPERBACK

A seductive game of hide-and-seek

Bethany Campbell

Nationally bestselling author of *See How They Run*

DON'T TALK TO STRANGERS

One by one the women were disappearing. Each had been young, vulnerable . . . and spending time "chatting" on the Internet with a mysterious stranger. It was Carrie Blue's job to track down that stranger, to put herself on the Internet in the guise of a lonely young student and smoke out a cunningly seductive killer. But soon she is drawn inexorably into a world where truth is indistinguishable from fiction . . . and it proves far more difficult than she could have imagined to resist the lure of a twisted mind—one that may already have figured out who Carrie is, and marked her as his next kill. . . .

"Carrie, look at me."

She struggled to keep control of her voice. "No."

"Yes," he said. "Are you afraid to? Why?"

She let her hands drop to her lap, straightened, and gave him a resentful glance. But she couldn't hold his gaze, and looked at the window instead, where the rain blurred the glass to a gray translucence.

"I know you were in the pub last night, alone," he said. "Then the Highwayman came in. You broke your connection, and he logged off immediately after. He never came back."

"How do you know all this?"

"I've learned a few tricks. I can see you from a

distance. Where you are and who you're with. But not what you're doing."

"You learned to do that from reading the archives?"

"Yes."

"You spy on me?"

"I monitor you and Brooke. Every fifteen minutes."

Carrie shrugged and said nothing.

"So what happened with the Highwayman?" he asked again.

"That's my business."

"It's my business too. There's a girl in a morgue in Illinois. Doesn't that matter?"

Her cheeks went hot and she shot him a glance of rebuke. "Of course it matters."

"So what about this Highwayman? What in God's name went on between you?"

Oh, hell, she thought wearily. If Hayden wanted the truth so much, she'd give it to him, right between the eyes. She no longer gave a damn about her pride, and it was Hayden who'd led her into this nasty farce.

"He was drunk. He wanted netsex. I said I wouldn't, not with someone who wouldn't tell me his name. So I broke the connection."

"I tried your private line," Hayden said. "It was busy. He phoned you?"

Carrie took a deep breath and told him what Paul Johnson had said. "I believe him. It makes me feel sick. This poor, disabled kid in love with a girl who doesn't exist. I want to hang myself."

Her chin trembled, and she thought, *I will not cry again. I will not let him see me cry. No one has seen me cry for ten years.*

Hayden's expression grew guarded. He might have been surprised or repelled, but all he said was "Carrie, Monica Toussant and Gretchen Small believed somebody too. What if it's not true? It's a damn good story. He loves you, and only you can heal him."

Carrie resisted the desire to pick up the coffee mug and fling it at his head. "If he's lying, he's contemptible. If he isn't, I'm contemptible. And if he's telling the truth, I couldn't stand it. The very thought makes me feel slimy."

He frowned. "He says his name's Paul Johnson? And he's not a citizen of the U.S.? How many guys do you suppose are named Paul Johnson in North America? He's got your phone number, but do you have his?"

"No," Carrie said. "So what?"

"He's living with a married sister, but you don't know her last name?"

She tilted her chin to a rebellious angle. "No."

"So how do you trace him, Carrie? How do you know he's for real? Do you have his address?"

"No," she said. "Stop trying to change my mind."

"I've got to. What if he's not some poor, disabled kid who thinks he's in love with you? What if he's an excellent liar who's stalking you?"

"What if he's not?" she challenged. "What if he's a twenty-three-year-old man who may never walk again? What then?"

"If we find out that's true, you let him down easy. It's not as if the two of you really know each other."

"He wants to have netsex with me, for God's sake. And I've encouraged him. I've let him hold me in his arms, hug me, kiss me."

He searched her face for a moment. Her confused emotions grew more tumultuous. *Something's going to happen*, she thought. *And I haven't got the strength to stop it.*

He said, "He's never touched you."

He put his hand to her face, his fingertips grazing first her cheekbone, then her jawline. With thumb and forefinger he lightly cupped her chin. "This is touching."

Her heart thudded crazily. She told herself, *Don't let this happen.*

"And he hasn't really kissed you," he breathed.

He tipped her face to his and brought his mouth to bear on hers, gently at first, then more hungrily.

Oh, God, oh, God, oh, God, she thought, her heart leaping.

He's real. He's real.

She had eight weeks to tame a savage—
and to fall in love.

LORD SAVAGE
by
Patricia Coughlin

The request was impossible. Unthinkable. And unavoidable.
Ariel Halliday couldn't refuse the head of the Penrose School
when he asked her to take on the particularly difficult as-
signment—not if she wanted to stay in his good graces. Now
she has only eight weeks to transform a savage raised on a
distant Pacific island into a gentleman. Yet nothing could
prepare her for the darkly handsome "pupil" who is the heir
apparent of the Marquis of Sage.

Ariel stepped inside the room and heard the door shut
behind her with a click that sounded as irrevocable as a
gunshot. She closed her eyes briefly, caught her breath,
and took a determined step forward.

"Good afternoon," she said. Another breath. In.
Out. She could do this. "I'm Miss Halliday. Miss Ariel
Halliday. I know that you're Leon Nicholas Duvanne,
the fifth Marquis of Sage. I'm just not sure that you
know it yet," she added ruefully.

She set the tray on the small table a few feet from
his cot.

"Of course you have a whole mouthful of other
titles I shall not even attempt to recite for you now. I
believe Lord Sav—Sage will suit nicely for the time
being."

Ninny, she thought. Such a slip of the tongue
might have made for a most uneasy moment. That is, if
he even understood a word she was saying. There was
still no indication he did. For that matter, there was no

obvious sign the man was alive, but for the slow, steady rise and fall of his very imposing chest.

Ariel, trying not to stare in fascination at the wedge of silky dark chest hair, wet her suddenly dry lips with her tongue.

"Proper manners," she began, "dictate that a gentleman rise when a lady enters the room and greet her by title and name. I am prepared to overlook your failure to do so on this occasion, overtaxed as I'm sure you must be from your obviously high level of exertion thus far today." He offered no response to her sarcasm.

"I do believe, however," she continued, "that in consideration of the fact that I have gone to considerable trouble to bring you tea, you could at the very least turn your head and acknowledge that I am speaking to you."

To her amazement, the dark head began to slowly turn her way. He understood, she thought excitedly. Either her words or her chilly tone, she couldn't be certain which, but he had clearly understood something. And he had responded.

Her excitement turned to apprehension as he proceeded to swing his feet to the floor and stand, facing her fully. She fought an urge to step back. He made no move to come closer, however, and her heartbeat gradually slowed to as near normal as she expected it to be while she remained confined there alone with him.

His gaze caught and held hers and Ariel found that the effect of his silent presence was even more daunting when he was staring directly into her eyes. He was, she concluded, without question the most beautiful man she had ever seen. Never before had she thought to describe a man as beautiful, but the word came to her easily and naturally when she gazed at Lord Sage's serene face and strong, lean body. He appeared to her as masculine perfection, chiseled by the hand of the greatest master of all.

His cheekbones were aristocratically high, his jaw

beneath the short black beard classically square, his mouth full, with just enough of a slant to add interest to his otherwise perfect face. A stray lock of his long, raven hair hung loosely across his forehead, and his eyes, deep-set and almond-shaped, were a quite extraordinary shade. Brown velvet swirled with gold, dark and bright at once, like sunlight on ancient brass. Tiger's eyes, Ariel mused, thinking of the gemstone by that name. Hard and gleaming and exotic.

At that moment the expression in his remarkable eyes was nether warm nor cold, neither friendly nor antagonistic. It was shuttered. She felt certain that the man was no dolt, and that although he would not permit her to be privy to it, there was a great deal of thought and evaluation going on inside his head. In fact, some instinct warned her that his lordship was taking her measure just as calculatedly as she was taking his.

She straightened, smoothing a few stray wisps of light brown hair. Why hadn't she taken more pains in arranging the chignon at the back of her neck that morning? she lamented. And perhaps worn a newer dress? One in a more flattering color? She quickly marshaled her thoughts, reminding herself that she did not possess a newer dress and that gray was a most serviceable hue for everyday wear and besides that, it mattered not at all what the man before her thought of her appearance.

Without warning he shook back his hair, dislodging the lock that hung over his forehead to reveal a two-inch-long scar there. The imperfection, which would have marred the appeal of most men, enhanced his instead. For the first time Ariel noticed the array of other small marks and scars that covered his body, souvenirs, it seemed to her, of a life far more reckless and exciting than her own. Feeling a mixture of curiosity and envy, she lifted her gaze to his to find him watching her with his eyes narrowed in suspicion.

The eagerly awaited reissue of a memorable classic
by

Sharon and Tom Curtis

LOVE'S A STAGE

Frances Atherton came to London to explore the plot that sent her father to prison. But she never imagined that she, too, would be held captive—by the charms of London's most scandalous playwright and fascinating rake. Devastatingly handsome Lord David Landry has charmed any number of women, and makes it clear that Frances is next. . . .

He had said there were two reasons he had been following her on Charles Street, the first being that he was concerned about her safely reaching her destination. It was true, Frances thought, that she might have had a difficult time locating her great-aunt's new address without him.

"But what was the second?"

"I beg your pardon?" he said, sending his sweet smiling glance at her.

"The second reason you followed me."

He looked, if not precisely surprised, then a little curious; he studied her face as if to revise a prior impression. His eyes were bright and kind as he said, "Miss Atherton, surely you must know."

The wind's mischievous fingers had loosened her bonnet strings. She retied them rapidly as she walked.

"Well, I don't. And as we've been walking along, it occurs to me to wonder why you would want to spend your time helping strangers around the streets, because I can see now, even if I did not at first, that you are quite a brilliant man."

It was his turn to be amused. "*Thank* you, Miss Atherton. You honor me too much. Do you know, though, that if you continue in that vein, I will find myself revising my previous estimate on the size of your hamlet downward. Hasn't anyone ever tried to seduce you?"

Seduce. She knew the word, of course, but it had previously played so minute a part in her vocabulary that she was forced to think a moment to recall its meaning. She gasped when she remembered and said simply, "No."

"That's quite an oversight on somebody's part." A crowded street corner was not the setting a man of his vast experience would have chosen to make a declaration of desire, nor was a bald statement of fact as likely to produce a successful result as were patience and attentive intimacy. To have ignored her direct appeal for an explanation, though, would have amounted to a deception alien to his nature.

A grin touched his lips as he noted they had arrived almost at the ornamental porch that marked the entrance to Miss Isles's apartments—at least, when she demanded the return of her case, she would have only a short space to carry it. "Miss Atherton," he said gently, "I would like to be more than friends with you."

Frances's young life had been devoted to duty and service. She was assistant mother to eight younger siblings, confidante and soul mate to her papa and aide-de-camp to her unworldly, domestically inclined mama. Excepting her brothers, the only young men Frances knew were the fishermen's sons from her village, any one of whom would have been too shy to woo the parson's lovely, intelligent daughter. There had been no proposals, proper or improper, in Miss Atherton's life, and while she might daydream in modesty of the former, it had never crossed her mind that she might ever be in a position to receive the latter. So unexpected was the declaration that Miss Atherton was not completely sure of his intention until he said helpfully, "Yes, Miss Atherton, I meant precisely what you think I meant."

To say that Frances was shocked would have been greatly to understate the case; in fact, she was astonished. She had never been encouraged to think of herself as pretty. As a result, she did not, and it came as a surprise to her that she could somehow have inspired those sentiments in any gentleman, particularly one who, it was quite obvious, could hardly have suffered from a lack of feminine companionship. Her incredulous surprise, however, was soon trampled by a flaming wrath.

"I suppose you think," she said dangerously, "that because I *allowed* you to talk to me on the street you can insult me!"

Capped in her shabby brown bonnet and cloaked in her puritanical morality, she had for him the quaint charm of a delightfully apt cliché. They had reached Miss Isles's building, so he set her case on the low porch before the door and took Miss Atherton's flushed cheeks leisurely between his palms, forcing her to look into his sparkling green eyes.

"Never, Prudence," he said with what Frances regarded as an odious tranquillity, "is it an insult to tell a woman that you find her so attractive that you would like to—"

Miss Atherton stopped his words by clapping her mittened hands over her ears in a gesture rendered unfortunately inefficient by the oversized contours of her bonnet. She removed her face from his hold with so forceful a back-step that if it were not for his steadying hands on her shoulders, she would surely have fallen.

"It is always, *al-ways*," she said furiously, "an insult unless preceded by a marriage vow."

Releasing her shoulders, he walked to the heavy

oak door and held it open for her. Miss Atherton marched past and found they had entered a narrow hall lined with marble wallpaper in yellow and brown. An interior door lay to the right of the entrance, and a wooden open-newel stair lit by a single lamp led to an upper landing. He lifted her case inside the threshold and shut the outer door behind them.

There was both rueful self-knowledge and compassion in his smile as he said, "That's one game I don't play, Prudence. I doubt if I'll ever be able to make that type of commitment to a woman. Honestly, sweetheart, there's very little chance I'd marry you."

Miss Atherton came to a full rolling boil. "Well, there is *no* chance that I would marry you!" She stormed to the door like a tidal wave and pounded against it with her fist.

On sale in December:

HAWK O'TOOLE'S HOSTAGE
by Sandra Brown

THE UGLY DUCKLING
by Iris Johansen

WICKED
by Susan Johnson

HEART OF THE FALCON
by Suzanne Robinson